I couldn't decide whether to laugh or dive in and ask more questions. On the one hand, telling me they were vampires, werewolves, faeries, and Greek gods was capital C crazy, but on the other, it was fascinating. What would make a group of kids act like this? Boredom, drugs, too many bad novels and movies? Then again, they seemed so serious about it all.

"So?" Tarren said, staring at me with those intense green eyes. "What are you?"

I decided at that moment to go undercover because the truth was, I hadn't had this much fun in months but I knew if I was going to stick it out with them, I would have to play along. "I'm a . . ." I glanced from person to person. Avis crossed his arms and stared hard at me. Johann frowned while I hesitated. "Werepire," I blurted out.

"A werepire?" Tarren said, drawing back. "Sounds like a word I would say."

"It's a mix," I told her, as if I were offended. "My mom's a shape-shifter and my dad's a vampire, so I'm a werepire."

They all looked at one another. "I've never heard of that," Tarren said.

"Can we interbreed?" Avis asked Johann.

"What powers do you have?" Helios asked me.

"None," I said. "Because of the cross-breeding. I'm like a mule."

OTHER BOOKS YOU MAY ENJOY

JOSIE GRIFFIN IS  A VAMPIRE

heather swain

speak

An Imprint of Penguin Group (USA) Inc.

SPEAK

PUBLISHED BY THE PENGUIN GROUP

Penguin Group (USA) Inc., 345 Hudson Street, New York, New York 10014, U.S.A. I Penguin Group (Canada), 90 Eglinton Avenue East, Suite 700, Toronto, Ontario, Canada M4P 2Y3 (a division of Pearson Penguin Canada Inc.) I Penguin Books Ltd, 80 Strand, London WC2R 0RL, England I Penguin Ireland, 25 St Stephen's Green, Dublin 2, Ireland (a division of Penguin Books Ltd) I Penguin Group (Australia), 250 Camberwell Road, Camberwell, Victoria 3124, Australia (a division of Pearson Australia Group Pty Ltd) Penguin Books India Pvt Ltd, 11 Community Centre, Panchsheel Park, New Delhi—110 017, India I Penguin Group (NZ), 67 Apollo Drive, Rosedale, Auckland 0632, New Zealand (a division of Pearson New Zealand Ltd.) I Penguin Books (South Africa) (Pty) Ltd, 24 Sturdee Avenue, Rosebank, Johannesburg 2196, South Africa I Penguin Books Ltd, Registered Offices: 80 Strand, London WC2R 0RL, England

First published in the United States of America by Speak, an imprint of Penguin Group (USA) Inc., 2012

10 9 8 7 6 5 4 3 2 1

Copyright © Heather Swain, 2012
All rights reserved
CIP data is available.

Speak ISBN 978-0-14-242100-0

Set in Candida
Designed by Irene Vandervoort

Printed in the U.S.A.

ALWAYS LEARNING   PEARSON

For Nora

JOSIE GRIFFIN
IS

A VAMPIRE

chapter 1

Josie Griffin?" The judge looked down her nose, over the rims of her small rectangular glasses. I popped up from my seat and sent my chair clattering backward.

"Yes, Your Honor," I said as sweetly and innocently as I could muster. Kevin must have been laughing his butt off, seeing me like this. A flowery blouse buttoned up to my chin and a skirt down below my knees. I had my nose ring out and my hair (its natural dingy blondish-brown again) pulled into a low ponytail, exposing the dots of sweat lining my forehead. I wouldn't give him the satisfaction of glancing his way, though. I was sure he was all slicked out in a jacket and tie like some young Republican. Jerk. *He has a fake ID and steals stupid things like potato chips and beef jerky and regularly buys pot from a guy in an ice-cream truck,* I wanted to yell. *And he should be slapped for how terrible he kisses!*

But of course, I didn't say any of that because my lawyer had warned me to be docile as a doorknob that day.

The judge glanced through her notes one last time, then she removed her glasses and stared at me. "Seems to me, Miss Griffin, that you've been a pretty good kid up until now."

I nodded and tried to look like the old version of me. The polite girl who was a cheerleader, the editor of the school newspaper, the straight-A student, the one who volunteered for Habitat for Humanity and organized bake sales for earthquake victims. The one my mom kept bemoaning got lost somewhere this summer after Kevin stomped on my heart and I stopped caring so much about the world.

"I guess you could call this a crime of passion," the judge said while glancing at Kevin's table.

Gag. I wanted to roll my eyes and say, *He wishes*, but I kept it to myself, something I should have done a month ago before I got myself into this mess.

She looked back at me. "Do you have anything you'd like to say to the court?"

I cleared my throat. Ms. Sheldon, my lawyer (who looked more like a hockey player in a pencil skirt than a legal professional), had prepared me for this moment and my parents made me rehearse it like a thousand times the night before as if I were prepping for the talent portion of a Miss Repentant American competition. *Chin up, Josie!* Mom would say. *Confident, but not so cocky. Try to look at least a little contrite.*

4

"Your Honor, I apologize for my actions," I said in my sweetest, most innocent voice, the one I'd used a million times to talk people into joining school committees or volunteering for good causes, or not grounding me when I broke curfew. "I know that I was wrong. I should not have bashed Kevin McDaniel's windshield in with a baseball bat. I was upset and emotional over his treatment of me, but that's no excuse for my behavior. This is the first time in my life I've ever been in trouble." Okay, so that wasn't *exactly* true, but technically I'd never been in trouble with the law, so my lawyer said it was okay to say it under oath. "And I promise you, it will not happen again. I've learned my lesson and I would like to get through my senior year without another incident so I can go to college."

Judge Levitz sighed and looked back down at her papers. "Very well. Judge rules you shall pay damages in the order of nine hundred and fifty dollars to Mr. McDaniel for repair to his car, plus court fees in the sum of fifty dollars. You shall also be on probation for one year and perform thirty hours of community service. If your record remains clean for one year, you may petition the court for expungement of the charges from your permanent record. However, to ensure that you can control your temper in the future I am sentencing you . . ."

I stumbled backward. *Sentencing me?*

". . . to six weeks . . ."

I gripped the chair behind me and nearly gasped. Was she sending me to juvie?

". . . of anger management group therapy."

I stood up straight. "Huh?"

The judge looked at me annoyed. "What's that?"

Ms. Sheldon grabbed my elbow. "Nothing, Your Honor," she said, squeezing my arm. "Thank you, Your Honor."

"Case adjourned," the judge said.

My mom threw herself at me as we headed into the hallway. "Oh thank god!" She sighed as she clung to me. "For a minute there I thought she was putting you in juvenile detention."

I tried to look unconcerned even though my heart had just started beating normally again.

"It's a little harsh," Ms. Sheldon said as she swung her raincoat around her broad shoulders and pushed us through the crowded hallway. "I didn't expect her to give you community service *and* anger management. One or the other I could understand, but both? Sheesh." She chucked me on the shoulder and I nearly tripped. "Sorry about that, kid."

How lame, I thought as I unbuttoned the top of my stupid blouse, which was about to strangle me. "Anger management therapy? Will I have to talk about my feelings with a bunch of hotheads?" I asked and Ms. Sheldon nodded. Oh well. At least it would be good material for JosieHatestheWorld, my blog where I chronicle all the crap that goes on in my life every day.

"Hey," my dad said. His forehead, which you could see more and more of those days, was bright red. "You ought to be grateful, missy. What you did . . ."

"I know, I know, Dad. Please. I've been through enough today." I untucked my shirt and loosened a few more buttons, exposing the white tank top I had on underneath.

"A thousand dollars! It had to be the '69 Camaro, didn't it?" He shook his head and I rolled my eyes because I was so sick of hearing about how I defaced a beautiful vintage Chevy as if it were a Renaissance sculpture. Whatevs. Kevin's daddy had a whole lot full of those stupid vintage muscle cars. "You will pay me back every red cent," my dad said.

"I know," I told him for the ten millionth time since I bashed in Kev's windshield.

"Jo. Hey, Jo." Kevin's voice came from behind me. I stopped and stiffened for two seconds, but I didn't turn around. I kept weaving through the other people in the hall toward the big red door to freedom. "Jo!" he called again. "Come on, babe."

The *babe* was what did it. I whipped around and pointed my finger at Kevin McDaniel's chest. "Don't you ever call me that again!" I spewed. Then I poked him in the sternum at every syllable. "I. Am. Not. Your. Babe."

He held up his hands and stepped back, probably afraid I was going to punch him next. He looked like an idiot with his blond hair parted to the side, wearing some stupid tan sports coat and blue and green striped tie—all of which I'm sure came right out of his father's closet.

"You look like a used car salesman," I told him with disgust.

He cocked an eyebrow at me. "And you look like yourself again."

"Bite me," I said, and just as I was about to turn around, I saw Madison peering out from behind him. She wore a body-hugging purple dress with a raggedy asymmetrical hem and black slashes across the front. "You!" I growled. "I can't believe you would have the nerve . . ."

"Josie, I . . ." Madison started to say, but I shot her the look of death and she shut her mouth.

"And in that dress!" I said.

She looked down at herself, smoothing the fabric over her hips. "What?"

"Zombie Apparel? We used to make fun of that store and all its Goth wannabe fashion victims." I rolled my eyes. "Then again, you never did have any originality. Which is why you had to steal my boyfriend instead of getting your own!" I stopped. It wouldn't do me any good to go after my ex-best friend right outside the judge's chambers.

"Come on, Josie." Mom caught my elbow and turned me toward the doors. "They aren't worth any more of your trouble. You'd only regret it."

Mom pulled me into the gray drizzle of that mid-

August day and I breathed in deeply. "I'm glad that's over." I raised my face to the sky, letting the moisture cover my cheeks.

"Me, too." Mom searched her bag for an umbrella. "I hope we never have to do this again."

While we stood there, Kevin and Madison came out the door. He had his arm around her shoulders and she leaned into him. They whispered together as they hurried down the courthouse steps toward another person standing at the bottom under a giant red golf umbrella. Chloe. Bee-yatch. My other ex-best friend who didn't have the courtesy to mention that Kevin and Madison were screwing around behind my back. The three of them huddled under the umbrella beneath one of the Zombie Apparel billboards that had sprung up like mold around the city in the past few months.

"God, I hate those ads," I said.

Mom opened her sensible brown umbrella to cover both of us. "Poor girls look emaciated," she said, studying the sickeningly skinny stick figures in the billboard, all hip bones and dark eyes under masses of long, tangled hair. The center girl in the ad wore the same dress Madison had on. Across the bottom of the billboard, scrawled like blood-red graffiti, were the words *Zombie Love Attack!*

A sharp barking noise, almost a laugh, leapt from my mouth. "It's the perfect caption, though, isn't it?" I had half an urge to snap a picture of my brain-dead ex-friends beneath that stupid catchphrase and post it on

9

my blog, but they crossed the street and climbed into Kevin's latest meathead muscle car plucked right off his daddy's lot.

"Nice car," my dad said and whistled through his teeth.

"God, Dad!"

He looked at me apologetically. "Sorry, Josie, but what do you expect? The kid is driving a mint late-60s Chevy Impala. You don't see many of those these days."

"I hope he wrecks it," I muttered, but as I watched them go, my chest hurt. I wouldn't cry, though. I pushed down that sadness and let it turn bitter in my gut. "You know what?" I said to my parents as the rain began to fall in quick sharp pellets. They both looked at me and waited. "I don't regret what I did for minute." My mom's mouth dropped open and my dad looked like I'd sucker punched him.

"Good god, Josephine!" Dad ran his hands through what remained of his hair. "Maybe you do need anger management therapy."

"Maybe so," I said as Kevin, Madison, and Chloe turned the corner out of my sight. I closed my eyes and remembered the aluminum bat in my hands. The way it thunked down on the trunk of his car as he scrambled out the passenger side door, yanking up his pants. I saw Madison's face, staring at me in horror from the back-seat. For just a moment I smiled as I remembered slamming the bat over and over onto the windshield. But my glee was short-lived because that feeling of the glass cracking into a thousand pieces under the weight of my fury was the same as the shattering of my heart that night.

chapter 2

My first act as a juvenile offender was to meet with my social worker one week after my court appearance. Since I was officially grounded until I hit thirty and school didn't start for another few weeks, I was almost looking forward to it. At least I'd have something new to say on JosieHatestheWorld.

"You are not wearing that," my mom groaned when I trudged through the dining room in my favorite short denim skirt with skull and crossbones patches on the butt, an old Siouxsie and the Banshees tee that my aunt gave me, and my best clunky black boots.

"What's wrong with it?" I said, looking down at myself. "I wasn't tried for fashion offenses."

Mom hopped up from the table where she was paying bills and waved her pen at me. "But, honey, you have to present yourself to your social worker as a person who's trying to change!"

"Why?" I asked, then I realized that she was probably talking about the purple streaks in my hair and the diamond stud in my nose. I had no intention of taking those out, so I smiled at my mom and said, "You're the one always telling me to be myself."

"That's true, but please just put on something presentable to meet with the social worker. Then wear whatever you want for the rest of the day." I could see the worry lines around her eyes. Lines my dad swore I'd personally etched onto her face in the past few months. "You can never take back a first impression, Josephine."

"Hmmm, where have I heard that one before?" I muttered, because that had become my mother's favorite refrain lately.

Mom tossed up her hands in exasperation, a gesture I'd also become very familiar with recently. "Just do it for me, would you?"

I felt bad, sort of. It wasn't like I was trying to antagonize my mom by looking like this. She just chose to be antagonized by how I looked. "Fine," I said in an effort to be a better daughter after what I'd put my mother through in court last week. "But I don't have time to wash the streaks out of my hair."

"Wear a headband," she called after me as I marched up the stairs.

In my room, I snapped a quick picture of myself, then I whipped off my boots, skirt, and T-shirt and rummaged around in my closet for a pair of khaki pants, a pale blue blouse, and brown flats—the uniform of Josie Past. I took another picture. I logged onto JosieHatestheWorld and uploaded both pix with a description of how Mom made me change from A to B for this meeting. Under picture B of me in my stupid khakis, I wrote, "I will not, under any circumstances, wear a headband!" I posted everything and logged off.

My blog had been my solace ever since Kevin and I broke up. It was the one place I could go to vent. And I went there a lot. I had another blog before the break-up called JosieRahRah. Old Josie liked to write about cheerleading camp and all my volunteer tasks and post pix of me and my "friends" (pardon me while I barf). I used to think I had so many things to post about. I was an A student, a great friend, a peppy cheerleader, editor of the school paper, and a stellar member of my community. I kept waiting for exciting things to happen for me.

But what did I expect? Awards? Accolades? Presidential Seals of Approval? Ha! Having my boyfriend and my best friend cheat on me while my other best friend knew it was going on wasn't what I had in mind. When it happened, I ditched JosieRahRah and started Josie-HatestheWorld. The irony being, I had so much more to say these days.

The good thing about starting JosieHatestheWorld was that I figured out what I want to do with my life. I always knew I wanted to be a reporter, but I used to think I'd be a TV news anchor or cover an art beat or something fluffy like that. But now I know that I want to be an investigative reporter. Like Graham Goren, a local journalist who's always uncovering political scandals and blowing the whistle on greedy corporations. If I had asked more questions, dug deeper, and followed my instincts that something was fishy between Kevin and Madison, I would have found out about them long before Chloe spilled her guts and I would have saved myself a lot of heartache. I vowed after that experience to never have my head in the sand again and to use my writing abilities to expose the injustices of the world someday.

On my way back downstairs, I sang, "I love you, Mom," and even though I might have sounded like a smart aleck, I meant it. I did love my mom. Even if she was annoying the crap out of me these days.

She looked up and nodded. "Much better," she said. "Call if you'll be late for dinner."

Gladys took a few minutes to warm up. You would, too, if you were a 1984 poop brown Honda Civic hatchback. She wheezed and coughed like an emphysema patient then creaked and shuddered as I eased her out onto the streets of Broad Ripple, where even the squirrels were polite. "Come on, old girl," I told Gladys, patting the dashboard. "You can do it, honey."

My car was so old it still had a tape deck. Which, by the way, I loved. How totally retro and weird was that? Kev kept trying to get me to buy a fancy new stereo, like what he had in his vintage car, or at least buy one of those thingies that can convert the tape deck to play MP3s, but I was a purist. If Gladys had a tape deck, I would listen to tapes. Luckily my aunt JoJo (yep, I'm her namesake) was a packrat and she bequeathed all her mixes from college to me so Gladys could sing. I popped in a mixed tape called *The Wall Came Tumbling Down* from 1989 when JoJo spent her junior year of college in London and the Berlin Wall fell. I sang along to New Order and The Smiths as I cruised toward downtown Indianapolis to meet Atonia Babineaux, my newly assigned social worker.

Driving through the perfectly parallel streets of Indy-no-place always reminded me that there was not a single interesting thing happening here. Never a diagonal for this grid-town. It was like someone drew a giant X over the state and put the capitol building where the lines intersected. Drew a circle around that building and called it "The Circle." Then radiated lines in ninety degree angles to one another from there. The streets were named after dead presidents (Washington, Jefferson, Madison) and states (Illinois, Michigan, Ohio). With the exception of Meridian Street, which bisects the city in half. Those street-namers were some creative geniuses.

Indianapolis is a poor excuse for a city, if you ask me, not that anybody did. Whenever I complained about Indiana, my dad liked to point out all the famous people who grew up here like James Whitcomb Riley, Tavis Smiley, and Garfield the Cat. Kurt Vonnegut being his favorite to harp on. But as I always pointed out to my dad, they all, even Garfield, left in the end. Which was exactly what I was planning to do as soon as I graduated. I'd blow this Popsicle stand and hightail it to the Windy City with Aunt JoJo where I'd go to University of Chicago (knock on wood that I got accepted) and study journalism. I couldn't wait to move to Chi-town. It was a real city with interesting people. I was just biding my time until I got there because, let me assure you, Indy had not one single interesting person. Not one.

Okay, so maybe there might have been one interesting person in Indianapolis. Or at least one very strange person and she was sitting right across from me. Atonia Babineaux was small, skinny, and extremely pale with short, spiky black hair and eyes so dark I swore I could see the moon in their centers. She was also a huge space cadet.

"It must be here," she mumbled, riffling through stacks and stacks of manila folders on her desk. "Somewhere. What did you say your name is again?"

"Josephine Griffin," I told her for the fourth time. "But I go by Josie." If the next six weeks of my life weren't in her hands, I might have found the whole scenario very amusing, but as it was, I was worried. "I had my court date last week. Maybe my file hasn't made it here yet."

She looked at me and blinked. I couldn't tell if she was an old person who looked young or a young person who looked old. "You're new," she said, and I nodded. "Why didn't you say so?"

"Um, I did. When I first got here," I told her, trying to keep the sarcasm out of my voice. First impressions!

Atonia grabbed a stack of paper from her in-box and flipped through all the sheets, muttering. "Gretchen, Gretchen, Gretchen."

"Excuse me," I said, trying not to be obnoxious, but this lady was causing me some serious anxiety. "You do know that my name is Josephine, not Gretchen."

She looked at me again as if I might be the one who was confused. "Really? Josephine?"

"Since I was born," I said.

"Well now . . ." She went back to digging.

While she was shuffling papers I took a good look around. Not that I thought being a juvenile justice social worker would ever be glamorous, but I was expecting a little more. Maybe a few "Hang in There" posters with kittens clinging to branches or pictures of mountain climbers exhorting me to "Reach for the Sky." This place was a dump. The green paint on the walls was peeling, the brown carpeting looked (and smelled) like vomit, and the one grimy window had a lovely view of a brick wall. Plus every surface overflowed with paper. I wondered what was in the filing cabinets—sandwiches?

Atonia slumped back in her chair. "I can't find you."

I raised an eyebrow at her. "I'm right here."

"Don't get cute, toots."

"Sorry," I mumbled. "I realize it's not your fault. Obviously somebody didn't send you the paperwork, it's just that I'm eager to get started with this whole community service and anger management thing so I can get it off my record. I'm about to start my senior year of high school and I don't want it to interfere with getting into college." See, Mom, I still had it. I could pander like a politician when I needed something. I leaned forward and gave her my best Josie-of-old smile. "Is there anything we can do to make this happen today?"

Maybe it was the khaki pants and the blouse or the way I was sweet-talking her, but whatever it was, Atonia shrugged. "Sure. Why not?" She grabbed a pad of paper and a pen off her desk and opened a big directory. "Anger management. Really?" She looked me up and down. "You don't look like the angry sort."

I just shrugged.

"What'd you do?" she asked while she flipped the pages.

"Bashed someone's windshield in with a baseball bat," I told her.

"Tsk, tsk," she said. "Naughty, naughty." She copied down some info onto a slip of paper. "Here's a group that meets this afternoon. Can you make it?"

Wait, let me check my social calendar. Right, I have no friends anymore and nothing better to do, so yeah, I guess I could make it. "Sure," I said, taking the paper from her. I squinted at the letters, barely decipherable, and asked, "What about my community service?"

"Hmm." She searched her desk again. She stuck her head under her desk and dug through a cardboard box full of junk. "Where did I put that directory?" I wondered if she'd ever heard of a fancy new contraption called a computer and that newfangled Internet they have now?

"Can't I just pick my own place?" I asked, because I was ready to get the H out of her office.

She looked up at me from somewhere around her knees. "Like what?"

"I used to volunteer for Habitat for Humanity. I could call them and see if they need my help."

"Nope, the place must be approved." She sat upright again and leaned back in her chair so far I thought she'd topple over. "Look, tell you what. You seem like a nice girl. I know a place that needs some extra help." She madly scribbled on another piece of paper. "It's a center called Helping American Girls."

"Seriously?" I asked, wondering if I'd heard her right. "You mean like the dolls?"

She looked up at me. "Are you making a joke?"

"Are you?" I asked.

"It's a shelter," she told me. "For runaway teen girls. I know the person who runs it and one of her workers just took a"—she paused and thought—"leave of absence. She needs some extra help for about a month." She shoved the paper at me. "Just make sure she signs this time sheet every week."

I nodded and said, "Thank you."

"You'd better hurry if you want to make that group," she said, pointing to the clock with her pencil. Then she laid her head down on her desk like she was going to go to sleep. "Give the therapist my note and I'll send the paperwork over later this week," she muttered with her eyes half closed.

I hopped up from my chair, mumbled thanks again, and I hightailed it out of her office.

chapter 3

When I got outside, dark clouds had gathered in the sky and the air was thick and warm like a whopping thunderstorm was about to break. Did I have an umbrella? No, of course not. That was one of the downsides of New Josie, she was almost always unprepared. Old Josie was so over-prepared that she practically carried a tent and cookstove with her everywhere.

But here's what I learned from being the one who always had my crap together: Everyone expects you to always have your crap together. Madison and Chloe always relied on me to make the plans—Josie will know the way. Josie will drive. Josie will make sure everyone gets where they need to go when they need to be there. Josie will have an umbrella. At some point, I got sick of always having the umbrella. Except for right then because big fat raindrops were falling on my head. I ran to

Gladys and jumped inside before the torrential down-pour began.

With the wipers squeeching and the defroster on, I drove around downtown Indy looking for the address scribbled on Atonia's paper. Every time I turned a corner, it seemed like I came face-to-face with another one of those stupid Zombie Apparel billboards. The models, like broomsticks with wigs, stared blankly in their urban-apocalypse-meets-soft-core-porn clothes with the words *Zombie Love Attack!* screaming at me. "Jeez, they're freakin' everywhere," I said.

The inside of my car was muggy, like the inside of somebody's mouth, and it smelled like bad breath. I guess chucking empty chicken quesadilla wrappers in the backseat wasn't the best idea if I wanted my car to smell like spring flowers. I pressed Ms. Babineaux's paper against the dashboard and squinted at the info again. It appeared to say 858 Illin or maybe that was 85 Chillin or maybe it was 2551 Linus or maybe it was in Swahili. I had only fifteen minutes until the meeting started, and despite New Josie's vow to never be early (that was an Old Josie habit) I didn't want to walk in on the middle of the session because then everyone would stare at me and . . . oh crap. That's when I remembered. Khaki pants! I was wearing flipping ugly khaki pants and a powder blue blouse like the cheerleader I used to be. Ugh. First impressions.

There was no way I was going into a room with a

bunch of juvenile delinquents looking like a total goob. I'd be eaten alive in no time. I pulled over to a parking meter on Illinois Street, killed the engine, and dove in the backseat. Surely I'd stashed some clothes back there at some point in the last few months. Lord knew there was enough junk to start my own personal landfill. I tossed aside take-out sacks, rummaged through piles of papers and books, pushed away empty cans and bottles until I uncovered a gym bag. Eureka! Inside were a pair of dark jeans, a black and white striped boater shirt, and some beat-up red Chuck Taylor shoes. Not exactly the look I was hoping for when meeting a bunch of tough kids, but it would have to do. I glanced around outside the car. The rain had emptied the sidewalks and fogged up my windows, so I hunkered down on the backseat to change clothes.

The next time I peeked out the window, I saw a guy under a black umbrella cocking his head to see inside my car. I zipped up my jeans and scowled at him. He was pale with shaggy brown hair and gray circles under his dark eyes. "What?" I yelled, which startled him. He grinned then hurried away. I watched him disappear inside a building half a block away. As I climbed into the front seat, I saw more people hurrying out of the rain, into the same building. A tall blond guy moved so smoothly it was like he was floating. Another guy with short dreadlocks standing on end kicked up his skateboard and held open the door for a petite girl who flipped a mass of bright red curls over her shoulder and smiled at him. They all looked about my age. I grabbed Atonia's paper from my dashboard and compared it to the address above the door. 2851 Illinois? Looked like I might be in the right place. I dashed out of my car, through the rain, and into the building.

The hallway was somber, like a morgue, the only noise the clicking of shoes somewhere ahead of me and the soft murmur of a few voices. I followed the sounds around a corner and saw the same group of kids filing into a room. My heart pounded and my stomach churned. I did not want to be there. I shouldn't have been there. I didn't have an anger problem. I could control my anger when I wanted to; I just didn't want to that one time and look where it landed me. It was so unfair.

These kids were probably real delinquents, although they looked harmless enough. But you could never tell. Sometimes the most ordinary looking people end up being the sickest. Look at Kevin. Everyone thought he was such an all-around good guy, Mr. Basketball, Tennis Captain, Class VP, leader of the young men's prayer circle by day. But by night, he was a total jerk. I knew for a fact that he and his friends would buy beer, shoplift snacks from a 7-Eleven, score some weed, and break in to empty houses to party, then they'd drive around harassing people or he'd end up at Madison's house while I was home studying or making pep rally signs like a blinded fool. So maybe the so-called "bad kids" were just the ones who got caught.

My plan was to slip into the room, take a seat in the

back, and listen like a journalist. Maybe I would even take notes and write about my experience on my blog. No matter what, I was going to keep my head down and do my best to make sure no one would notice me. Except that when I got inside I saw that a) the chairs were arranged in a circle and b) the only one not occupied was at the opposite end of the room and c) that chair was beside the creepy peeper guy who looked inside my car. Great. Of course, since I was the new girl, everybody stopped what they were doing and stared at me. I felt like a bunny hopping through a fox's den. I walked quickly with my head down, hoping they'd lose interest in me if I appeared uninteresting.

When I got to the open seat, the creepy peeper looked up at me, raised an eyebrow, and flashed me a cheesy grin. I rolled my eyes at him and plopped down in the seat.

The last person through the door was clearly the therapist. He was probably my dad's age with a full beard and short sandy gray hair. He wore pressed plaid pants and Hush Puppies shoes that were almost silent on the linoleum. He glanced around the circle, nodding to each person until he got to me and looked startled. "Ah, a new addition to our happy little group?"

Nothing like stating the obvious. I stood up and handed him the note from Atonia. "Ms. Babineaux said I could join you starting today."

"Who?" he asked.

"My social worker. She'll send over the rest of the paperwork later."

He studied Atonia's scrawl for a moment with a frown then he shrugged. "Okay, well then, I'm Charles, the facilitator of this group. Welcome, Josephine."

"Josie," I corrected him.

When I sat down the creepy peeper guy leaned way too close. He stared at me intensely as if he thought he could hypnotize me. "That's a very sexy name, Yosie," he said. There was something so dorky about that guy. Maybe it was the haircut, a little too long in back and frizzy in the front. Or his clothes, a short satiny jacket with big shoulders over a paisley shirt, as if he'd stepped out of one of those bad 1980s movies Aunt JoJo loved so much. Or maybe it was his voice, annoying and nasally with a weird accent I couldn't place. Russian or Slavic or something.

"A) it's Josie," I said, leveling my gaze at him. "With a *J*."

"That's what I said," he told me with his eyebrow cocked again. "Yosie." He locked eyes with me and seemed to anticipate something, like he was waiting for me to swoon.

But I was far from swooning. "And b)," I said, "ew."

He turned away sheepishly and I heard someone snicker from across the room.

"Okay," the therapist said. "Let's jump right in. How's the week been? Who wants to start?"

The dreadlock guy lifted his hand. "I'll go," he said. As I watched him talk, I realized he was seriously cute with piercing gray-blue eyes and dark skin under the layers of short red-tinted braids snaking from his head like tendrils from a plant. He was lean but I could tell he was muscular under his baggy jeans and tee. "It was a full moon, so you know, that made my week tougher," he said, and I thought, *Oh brother.* The moon made his week hard? Sounded like Aunt JoJo when she went through her New Age Wicca stage ten years ago. She was always talking about how the mother moon's ebb and flow dominated her cycle. Happily she no longer bought into that malarkey. I would have never pegged this guy for a New Age moon worshiper, though. Looked more like a skate rat to me.

"Can you share what happened, Avis?" Charles asked.

Avis squirmed in his seat, poking his head forward again and again like a bird. "Yeah, so I was skating with some of my homies around the Circle and the cops started giving us a hard time, for no good reason. We weren't doing anything wrong. No jumping or trying to ramp the steps or ride the rails. The cops were just bored, probably. Didn't have any real criminals to go arrest, so they were harassing us. I could feel my anger coming, you know, like it was bubbling up under the surface. Like my skin was going to split open and unleash the beast. And it was crazy intense because the moon was shining down on me like a spotlight, man, and part of me wanted to attack one of those doughnut-munching pigs."

Dang, unleash the beast within? I got mad and all, but I never felt like I was going to pop out of my skin and rip a cop's face off.

"How did you deal with that? Did you use any of the strategies we've discussed?" Charles asked.

Avis sat back in his chair, eyes darting side to side. "I took some deep breaths and I walked myself through our questions. I asked myself why I felt angry. I asked myself why I wanted to lash out at the cops. And I reminded myself that letting things get ugly is not in my best interest."

"Did that stop you from acting out?" Charles asked.

"Yeah, but I was still pissed," Avis said. "So I took off on my board. I just went all out and pumped as hard as I could down Meridian, racing cars and blowing through stop lights."

Charles frowned. "Was that a good choice?"

Avis's laugh was strained, like one of those rubber chickens you squeeze. "Well, it was better than the alternative."

"Yes," Charles said. "You've got a point."

"See, this is what I don't get," the redheaded girl said. She sat next to Avis with her knees drawn up toward her chest. She was a tiny thing with skinny little arms and legs but she seemed to buzz with energy, like she could levitate off the chair any minute. Maybe it was all the crazy waves of bright red hair that cascaded down her back or how her green eyes flashed while she tried to get the words out, which seemed stuck behind her lips for a moment. "We're not the emeny!" she said passionately.

Emeny? I looked around but no one else seemed bothered by this.

"That stuff is deep inside our, our, our, you know." She paused and thumped her chest with her fist. "Seep in our douls, I mean, deep in our souls! So why is it a crime?"

Charles sighed, as if they'd been over this a million times before. "It's not a crime to feel anger, Tarren. It's only a crime if you act on it in a way that hurts others."

Tarren flapped her arms around her head and talked fast, like she was about to fly away. "Yeah, but we're made to feel guilty because of who we are and how we experience the world. As if there is only one way to be."

She had a point, I thought. It was like my how my parents thought I couldn't simultaneously streak my hair purple and pierce my nose and still be a decent human being. Those things *could* coexist.

"Would anyone else like to address Tarren's comment?" Charles asked.

The blond guy signaled with a slight nod of his head. I turned my attention to him and nearly fell off my chair. I don't think I'd ever seen a more beautiful boy. It was as if the sun shone from behind his skin. His hair was a mix of every blond you could imagine from the dusty yellow of corn husks to the white of fresh snow and his eyes were gold. He also had the most perfect nose I'd ever seen. It was strong and straight with the nostrils slightly flared as if he was drinking in all the scents the world had to offer. Somehow his face almost looked familiar—those deep set eyes and chiseled cheeks, as if I'd seen him a hundred times before, but I couldn't quite place him.

"This is the world we were born into," he said. "It's not something we can change, so we have to accept it and deal with it the best we can."

"Easy for you to say, Helios," Tarren muttered.

He turned to her and flared his nostrils more. He looked like a statue of an ancient warrior about to go into battle. "What makes you think it's easier for me?"

Tarren shrugged. "Not all of us were born with that golden cherry-thingie. Whaddya call it? That thing he drives?"

"Chariot," Avis told her.

"That was one of my great-great-grandfathers," Helios said drily. "I drive an Infiniti."

"Whatever it is," Tarren said. "I'm stuck on the Southside with a drunk for a father and a mother who flits in and out while I'm forced to go to some crappy school, but Helios here glides around Carmel to his fancy private school. I think I have more of a right to be pissed off than he does."

I sat back. I knew I should keep my mouth shut. Tarren might have been little and she might have talked weird, but she could kick somebody's butt and I didn't want it to be mine. But, I couldn't do it. "Money doesn't necessarily make life easier," I said.

Tarren glared at me. "Spoken like a true princess."

I snorted. "Hardly."

Charles chimed in. "I think the point is we're all entitled to feel anger or frustration, no matter how much money we have or don't have. Rich, poor, or in between we all have problems that are worthy of consideration."

I glanced over at the blond guy, expecting a nod of appreciation or something, but he ignored me.

"Let's move on," Charles said. "How about you, Johann?" He turned to creepy peeper guy. I felt a little bad for making fun of how he said my name, since his was pronounced Yohann. He was probably some poor foreign kid whose family left a war-torn country and I was giving him a hard time. Maybe my dad was right. Maybe I did need therapy.

"What can I say?" Johann sighed like a weary old man. "I'm bored. I'd like some excitement in my life." He shook his head and I felt his pain. Who wouldn't like a little more to do in this town?

I must have been nodding in agreement because Charles looked at me and said, "Do you feel that way as well, Josie?"

"I, uh, um, yeah, I guess so," I sputtered.

"Tell us a little bit about yourself," Charles said. "What brings you here today?"

Uh-oh, I thought. I can happily listen to other people

talk about their lives for hours. I can write about anything under the sun. I can even defend a position if I
think it needs defending. But talking about myself? Out
loud? No thank you, I'd rather pass.

chapter 4

Charles wouldn't let me off the hook, so I took a deep breath. Over and over I had had to relive how I'd completely lost it on Kevin's car. By now my explanation had become rote and mechanical and included just the barest of details. "I got angry and bashed in someone's windshield."

Everyone stared at me, waiting.

"It was my boyfriend."

They continued staring. I squirmed under the heat of Helios's eyes.

"He was cheating on me," I added but that didn't break the silent let's-all-look-at-Josie game.

"With my best friend, okay? I caught them and it pissed me off."

Everyone's eyes shifted around. They glanced at one another and no one seemed to breathe.

Charles cleared his throat. "Josie," he said, leaning

forward. "You do understand that this is a safe place, right?"

I had no idea what he was talking about but I sort of nodded anyway.

"You will not be persecuted here," he said.

"Don't hold back," Tarren told me. "This is the one place that nobody will come at you with a stake for being who you are. Even if that's a rich princess."

That made Johann laugh but I was annoyed. "First of all, I'm not rich," I told her. "And why would anyone come at me with a T-bone?"

"What they're trying to say," Avis told me, "is that it's okay to admit the whole story."

I thought about this for a moment. But that was the whole story. Sure, I could have gone on and on about how I really thought I had been in love with Kevin. How his good boy/bad boy dual personality thing seemed interesting rather than schizo and I was sure if I just tried hard enough to be the perfect girlfriend, the good boy in him would love me back. How I knew now that I was an idiot but I should have seen it coming that he was screwing around with Madison. Only I didn't, so when Madison told Chloe everything and Chloe finally let the truth slip, it tore a hole in my heart the size of a meteor crater and all those years of being good, sweet, quiet Josie who let the world walk all over her exploded out of me with a rage I didn't know I was capable of. But I didn't see how that was anybody's business, so I kept my mouth shut.

"In due time," Charles said. "It takes a while to build

up the trust. Josie will confide in us when she's ready."

Fat chance, I thought.

"Let's go back to Avis," Charles suggested. "Did you morph on the night you were angry with the police?"

Avis did that birdlike head jutting thing again. "But I was careful this time, chief. Just like you taught me. I rode up to Hollis Park. I stayed in control until I hit the woods. I made sure no one was around. I picked a specific place to shed my clothes, like you suggested, and then I let the change happen. And I ran. I just ran, you know? I had to get it out of my system."

Um, did I just imagine it, or did that guy admit to streaking naked through Hollis Park at night?

"What happened when you came back?" Charles asked.

"I had stayed inside the park this time. And I didn't hurt anything. Just chased a few squirrels, maybe a rabbit or something," Avis said.

Okay, the dude chased squirrels while he was naked? All I did was hit a car with a bat.

"So, when I came back, I was tired and a little disoriented, but I had enough energy left to find my clothes and my skateboard and get myself home safely."

Charles smiled big. "That's wonderful progress, Avis. I believe the last time you morphed, you were admitted to the psych ward."

My mouth dropped but Avis just snickered. "Yeah, something about a naked black kid wandering around a Target parking lot at two a.m. doesn't sit well with the community. They locked me up so fast I didn't have time to spit." He crowed that weird loud laugh again, which almost made me giggle.

Everyone else laughed, except for Tarren. She reached over and laid her hand on Avis's arm. "That's what inferiorates me," she said. "We're not mentally ill."

Okay, Tarren, whatever you say, but people who chased squirrels in the nude qualified as a little bit kooky in my opinion.

"Do you sometimes feel like people think you're crazy?" Charles asked.

"Only when I act like myself," Tarren said and once again, despite how strange she was, I found myself agreeing with her.

"Can you give me an example?" Charles asked.

Tarren rearranged herself in the chair so she was sitting cross-legged like a yogi. She leaned forward and spoke intensely, using her hands to illustrate every word. Even though she kind of scared me, I was fascinated by her. She looked like a pretty little doll I would have wanted to play with when I was six, but she was fierce.

"Okay, so last week at school this guy was giving me a hard time. He's one of those jumb docks; I mean, dumb jocks who thinks every girl wants him in her pants and for some reason he's zeroed in on me, only I'm not going to take it. I'm not some little bambo who's going to laugh at his stupid, retrograde jokes."

I blinked and stared hard at her, trying to puzzle through what she was trying to say.

She lowered her voice and added a thick southern accent, "'Hey, baby, if I told you you had a great bod, would you hold it against me? Huh-huh-huh.'" Then she said in her regular voice, "As if that's some giant turn on."

I blushed as Tarren spoke so matter-of-factly about sex. Maybe she had some kind of addiction or something because I could never have said those things to a group of near strangers.

She continued without the slightest embarrassment. "So he follows me one day after school, right? Gets on the same, you know, thingie." She motioned doors opening and closing.

"Bus?" Avis guessed.

"Yeah, he gets on the same bus as me, gets off at my stop, even though I know he doesn't live near me. Walks behind me as if he just hangs around long enough I'll be like, 'Hey, horn dog, let's get it on!'" She shook her head. "Look, I told him to back off. I gave him fair warning."

Very calmly Charles said, "And then what happened?"

"Well, he pushed the issue," she said. We all looked at her.

Only Avis spoke. "Exactly how did he push it, Tare?" His words were low in his throat and his hands gripped the edge of the desk while he puffed up his chest. Tarren reached over and stroked his arm. I wondered if they were a couple.

"I mean it literally. He pushed me down an alley

and against a wall. Telling me that I've been asking for it and that I'm going to like it."

"This is not a new experience for you," Charles said.

"Same old, same old in my neighborhood," Tarren said, and I shrank in my chair, afraid to listen to the rest because she was so tiny and I couldn't imagine how she could have gotten out of the situation. But a small grin spread over Tarren's lips. It was a smile I recognized. She felt the same way I felt when I smacked the crap out of Kevin's car. So wrong, but oh so right.

"And?" Charles prodded her.

I leaned forward, curious to hear what Tarren did.

She shrugged and laughed. "I turned him into a dog."

Everyone cracked up but me and Charles. I was still trying to figure out what she meant. Was that code for kicked him in the balls? Charles rubbed his face like he was exhausted and didn't know what he was going to do with Tarren. I couldn't blame him.

"Don't worry, Chucky," Tarren said with a perky grin on her face. "It was temporary and nobody saw me. We were in an alley. He scampered off. I'm sure he came to while digging through a pile of trash or treeing on a pea."

Treeing on a pea? I tried to translate this in my head. *Peeing on a tree, maybe?*

"Tarren," Charles said firmly. "This is exactly what we've been trying to work on in here. Finding other solutions so you don't end up with more problems."

"What was I supposed to do?" Tarren erupted, arms and legs flying until she was nearly hovering over the little desk attached to the front of her chair. "He had me cornered. I didn't do anything to provoke him other than be myself. I even warned him. Was I supposed to let him molest me? Is that fair? How many times do I have to be punished by society for being born this way? I had to defend myself!"

I didn't know what to think. On the one hand, I agreed with her. On the other hand, she was clearly bonkers if she thought she turned some jerk into an actual dog. Maybe she was repressing her memory of the attack. Or maybe she was just out of her mind.

Charles shook his head. "What happened the next time you saw him?" He sounded exasperated. "Did he seem to remember?"

Tarren rolled her eyes at him. "I'm not an amateur, Chucky," she said. "I cast a memory hex in the spell. All he knows is that he shouldn't mess with me again."

"You know I have to report it to the Council," Charles said and everyone groaned.

"It's not fair," Avis said.

"Whatever happened to whaddya call it—infidelity between doctors and patients?" Tarren muttered.

Charles stopped writing. "I believe you mean confidentiality."

"Yeah. What about that?" she asked.

"You know the rules," he said, jotting notes again. "No details, but the Council has to know of any incident."

"Then why aren't you reporting Avis?" Helios asked.

Charles rubbed his eyes and looked weary. I almost felt sorry for the guy. "I don't want to bust your chops," he said. "I'm trying to help you guys move on with your lives. But Tarren hexed that young man in broad daylight on a city street. There could have been witnesses. The incident could have been reported by the public so I have to report it. But no one was around when Avis morphed, so that information won't leave this room."

"Unless Helios runs and tells his mommy on me," Avis said with a snort.

Helios blinked. "As Charles said, nothing leaves this room."

"Except for that," Tarren pointed to Charles's paper.

Charles seemed helpless for a moment. "I don't make the Council rules, Tarren. But I do have to follow them. I'm sorry. The bottom line, my friends, is that these are the years in which you make the transition from child to adult. Your bodies are changing, your powers are growing. Eventually you will be independent. Your parents, and the Council, want to make sure you are prepared to live in society as productive, useful citizens. That's why we take great lengths to prepare you. Sometimes it may feel like we're hovering, but we're only concerned with your well-being."

Then he stopped and looked around at us slumped in our seats. He shook his head. "It's hard for you guys to understand, but fifty years ago, our kind didn't get to live in society like this. We were underground and hunted. There were no safe havens. We had no rights. I don't know how to convince you, but the arrangement the Council has made with the state, and even Saskatchewan, is beneficial for all of us. It's up to you to keep it in good standing."

Whoa! *The Council?* What council? The one on Insane Juvenile Delinquents and their Nutball Therapists? This whole group was whack. Charles glanced at his watch. I wondered if it was almost time for the paddy wagon to come pick up the lunatics. What really concerned me was whether Charles thought I was one of these delusional freak shows. Clearly I didn't belong with these people.

"Whatevs," Tarren said with a shrug.

Avis, who was relaxed back into his chair again, smiled at Tarren and patted her shoulder. "Don't worry about it, baby. You did the right thing."

"No," Charles said. "She did not do the right thing. Let's be clear about that. Casting spells to get yourself out of trouble is the wrong thing. And had you been caught, the consequences would be severe. You jeopardize every one of us when you take such risks."

At that moment I was sure I was in the wrong place because not only did Avis and Tarren think they had some sort of supernatural powers, but Chucky was buying what they were selling. Despite the fact that I was sort of freaked out by the whole experience, I was also completely fascinated. I wished I could ask questions and take notes. Mom always said it was a good thing

I wanted to be a reporter because at least then I'd get paid for my curiosity. So, rather than trying to get up and leave, I sat back and listened, sure that later I'd have an awesome post when I wrote about this on my blog.

"He's right, you know," Johann said. Everyone turned toward him. "The rest of us control ourselves. It's not easy but we do it and you should, too."

Avis reared up again. "Back off, Yo!"

"Why should I?" Johann asked, as calm as could be. "I control my urges. How long has it been since I've had a fresh kill?"

I nearly jumped out of my seat. What the hell kind of group was this? Was I sitting next to a teenage serial killer?

"Pasteurized blood tastes nothing like the real thing, and yet I drink it. Day after day. Ugh."

"Fourteen weeks," Tarren said. Everyone stared at her.

"Since the horse?" Helios asked.

She nodded with a satisfied smirk.

Johann shook his head and waved his hands. "It was just a horse."

"A police horse," Avis said. Tarren giggled.

"It was sickly. I was putting it out of its misery," Johann said.

"Wait a sec," I said, because I couldn't take this anymore. "You killed a horse?"

Johann shrugged at me. "It was a moment of weakness," he explained. "And I've been clean since then." He glanced at Charles. "Only four more weeks and I'm free, no?"

Charles looked skeptical. "Technically, yes, if you keep your nose clean."

"Or should you say, keep your fangs clean?" Tarren asked. That killed Avis. He doubled over, cackling.

"Listen, faerie girl," Johann said, "I've not touched a human . . ."

"Don't talk to her like that," Avis snapped.

"Yeah, don't talk to me that way," Tarren said. "Just because you're undead doesn't mean I can't zap you."

Undead?

"I can smell your blood from here," Johann warned. Avis hopped up, one foot on his seat, the other on the desk as if he were ready to leap, only his feet got tangled up and he fell face first toward the floor where he landed sprawled at Helios's feet. Like a flash of lightning, Helios vaulted over the back of his chair and crumpled into a ball on the floor while Avis and Johann stood nose to nose with their fists balled at their sides. While the two of them stared at each other, the lights flickered overhead as if there were a sudden power surge.

I was riveted to my seat, half scared and half dying to see what the lunatics would do next. It was like a movie, only real. Would they actually get in a fight?

"Enough!" Charles yelled. He was out of his seat, arms above his head, and just at that moment, a giant clap of thunder rattled the windows. "Each of you calm down before I have to restrain you." His voice boomed nearly as loud as the storm outside.

I looked around the room, wondering if anyone

44

other than me was sane. My eyes landed on Helios who'd slipped back into his seat and calmly examined a hangnail, as if he was bored with the whole ordeal. Maybe this happened all the time. Whether it did or not, Charles's threat had diffused the situation. Avis took a few breaths and got back into his chair, but he never took his eyes off Johann who stared steely daggers back at him.

"Let's use this as a learning event," Charles said. "Breathe deeply." Everyone but me joined together on an inhale while Charles counted to four, then they all exhaled together. I felt like I was in a yoga class. Were we going to salute the sun next? "Do you see what this kind of anger does?" Charles asked. "It tears us apart. And we can't afford to have factions."

Then he turned to me. "And on Josie's first day here. What must she think of us?"

Johann bowed deeply toward me. "My deepest apologies, Yosie." He reached for my hand. I tried to squirm away but his grip was strong. He lifted my hand toward his mouth and laid a strangely cold kiss on my skin. "I am ashamed of my behavior."

"Yeah, um, no sweat," I said, wrenching my hand away from him and wiping it on my jeans.

"We wouldn't really hurt each other," Tarren said. She reached out and patted Johann's shoulder. "I mean, we get pissed off at each other and vent sometimes, but really, we're a big happy family."

"Or fappy hamily, as you once called us," Johann

said and slipped his arm around her tiny shoulders.

She laughed. "I did say that, didn't I?"

"Truth is," Avis said, "we've got each other's backs and what happens in this group stays in this group."

Everyone around the room nodded.

"Josie, can you share with the group what you're feeling?" Charles asked me.

"Well." I squirmed, wondering if it was impolite to point out to crazy people that they're crazy. "No offense. This has been a fascinating experience and all, but I don't think this is the right group for me."

"And why is that?" Charles asked.

"Oh well, you know. The time isn't a great match for my schedule and . . ." I started to stand up. Curious or not, I thought I'd be better off with a group of kids who weren't nutso.

"Josie?" Charles looked intently at me. "What are you?"

"What am I doing?" I asked, uncertain. "I'm leaving."

"That's not what I asked," Charles said. "I asked, what are you?"

My eyes darted around the room at the others watching me. I could tell them what I wasn't. I wasn't a girl who thought she could turn jerky guys into dogs and I wasn't a guy who went running naked through a park chasing squirrels and I would never kill a horse. "I'm just a girl," I said quietly. "An ordinary girl who got a little pissed off and lost my temper one day." I felt like

46

shrinking now. Ever since Kevin, Madison, and Chloe betrayed me, I thought I had the biggest problems in the world. I tried to pretend I was tough and could handle anything. But compared to everyone here, I might as well have gone back to the cheerleading squad.

"Would anyone like to say anything to Josie?" Charles asked.

Helios was the only one who spoke up. "It took each of us a few sessions to feel we could expose what we've hidden for so long. At times it is difficult. We've spent so many years covering, but once you allow yourself to open up here, it will be worth it."

The others nodded in agreement.

"Despite what you just witnessed, I can assure you that you are safe here," Charles said. Then he glanced at his watch. "Oops! Time's up." He gathered his papers and smiled at everyone. "I think we made some progress today."

chapter 5

Outside, the rain stopped and the clouds were moving off toward the east so that the early evening sun illuminated the empty office buildings surrounding us. Downtown Indy was dead after five o'clock when all the little office drones headed for their big screen TVs in the burbs. The only person I saw was a homeless guy rooting through a trash can across the street.

As I fished for my car keys, Tarren walked up and said, "We always go out afterward. You want to come?"

"It would be delightful if you joined us, Yosie," Johann said, giving me that half-creepy stare like he thought he could change my mind.

Helios walked up. My eyes wandered to his lips. What would it be like to kiss someone that gorgeous? "We can go somewhere nearby," he said.

I liked the *we* in that sentence, so I nodded and said, "Okay, I'll tag along." Because whether these kids were crazy or not, who in their right mind would pass up an opportunity to hang out with smoking hot Helios?

"You want to go to Buffy's?" Tarren asked.

"Ugh, always with the Buffy's," said Johann.

"Come on." Tarren smacked Johann's back. "It's fun, plus the southwestern cheddar poppers are jamming."

"Anyway what do you care what we eat?" Avis asked and held his hand up for a high five from Tarren.

"Let's go," Avis said and grabbed my arm. "This self-awareness BS makes me hungry!" Then he looked to the sky, and I swear to god, he crowed.

Okay, forget what I said about Indy being boring. Turned out, I was hanging out with the wrong people. If you're a certifiably insane juvenile delinquent, the town was popping. Take Buffy's, for example. How did I not know it was there? Because to get to it you had to go through a nondescript parking garage on Jefferson, down three flights of stairs, over a cement retaining wall, and through an unmarked door, that's why.

Once we got inside, Johann was quickly surrounded by a league of super skinny girls dressed head to toe in Zombie Apparel atrocities. Short shorts over black fishnet stockings with plunging see-through V-necks over ripped-up tank tops—exactly the look half the cheerleaders were trying to cop this summer. Ugh. But, for a guy who nearly gave himself a hernia hitting on me, he was surprisingly uninterested in the Zombie Love Attack! taking place around him. The delegation of Johann lovers whispered in his ear and clung to him like ants on a stick but he extracted himself from their lair and sidled up to me instead.

"What's with the love zombies?" I asked.

He laughed. "Ah, love zombies! That is a funny one, Yosie. That is what I will call them from now on. You are very delightful." He grabbed my hand and planted another cold, dry kiss on my knuckles. I wrenched it away. Then he leaned against the counter where the crowd ordered sodas, energy drinks, and coffee from three baristas dressed all in white. Johann leered at me and said, "Would you like to dance, Yosie?"

"Dance?" I didn't know whether to be grossed out or to laugh.

"Perhaps the rumba or a tango." He pressed one hand against his belly and swiveled his hips in the most nauseating way. "Or do you like the disco?" He struck a pose and I nearly threw up in my mouth.

"Johann, are you for real?" I asked.

"What do you mean, am I for real?" He looked a bit wounded.

"It's just that everything you say and do make it seem like you're trying to hit on me and the way you look at me . . ."

"Do you feel my power?" He gave me the cheesy, one-eyebrow-up grin.

"Look, Johann, no offense. I know we just met and all, but it ain't going to happen."

His shoulders slumped.

"What's the prob, homie? Lady troubles again?" Avis asked, slapping Johann on the back. Then he handed me some kind of iced mochaccino concoction with whipped cream. Yummy.

Avis flashed me a knowing grin. "Don't take Yo too seriously, Josie. He can't help being on the prowl."

"Ack, what good does it do me?" Johann shrugged his shoulders in a way that reminded me of my grandfather. "In the old country, at the discotheques, I had the women eating out of my palm." He stopped with a gleam in his eyes.

"Mind games," Avis said with a knowing glance, only I couldn't imagine Johann being slick enough to mess with anyone's mind.

Then Johann sighed and waved his hand dismissively. "But with you?"

I licked whipped cream from my lips. "Dude," I said. "What about all the other girls in here?"

"Meh," he said with a shrug.

"Or the love zombies?" I pointed to the skinny club who sat staring blankly at Johann from across the room. "Go dance with them."

He nearly shuddered. "No thank you."

"Who are they?" I asked.

"Messed up, that's who," Avis said with a cackle.

I followed Avis and Johann to a table where the rest of the group dug into baskets of deep fried goodness. "We didn't know what you'd like," Tarren said, "so we ordered one of everything to share."

I grabbed a stool and pulled it between Helios and Avis. "Thanks," I said, loading up a plate with fried mushrooms, French fries, some kind of puffy cheese ball things, and what appeared to be deep fried mini Snickers bars. Johann sat across from me, looking glum and not eating a thing while everyone else snarfed down the snacks.

"Do any of you have to do community service?" I asked between bites.

"Ah, yes," Helios said. "The rehabilitation model. Criminals should be cured rather than punished. It's as old as Plato himself."

Seriously, if the guy weren't so freakin' hot, he would have been a total dork.

"We all have to do it," Tarren told me. "It's supposed to make us more a part of the upworld community, so we're not lurking down here, getting ourselves into trouble."

I glanced around. This hardly looked like the kind of place anyone could get in trouble. There was music playing, some video games, a small stage in the back, and lots of kids just hanging out talking, eating, laughing.

"What did you get stuck with?" Avis asked while picking at some tempura veggies.

"Some place called Helping American Girls," I said with a snort. "Sounds like a rehab center for dolls doing drugs."

The others laughed but Tarren frowned. "I know that place," she said. "It's in my neighborhood."

"What's it like?" I asked.

"Creepy," she told me. "I get whaddya call it—like bad static from the woman who runs it."

"Can't be any worse than my social worker," I said. "She was a nut. Her office was a total wreck. She didn't even have a computer. I was like, 'Ever heard of the Internet, lady?'" They all looked at me kind of funny. "What?"

"You mean you want your record computerized?" Tarren asked.

"Er, uh, I don't know. Just seems easier than all the paper," I said. Then I mumbled, "She wasn't very organized," and I wondered if I sounded like Old Josie who prized organization and neatness above all else.

"But the Council fought so hard for our records to be kept off the Internet," Tarren said, like I was a total jerk for suggesting otherwise.

"Why?" I asked. "What have you got against the Internet?"

Avis shook his head. "I don't know about you, but I don't need racists and demon hunters after me."

"Demon hunters!" I said and groaned because Kevin and his friends were the kinds of idiots who trawled the Internet for stupid stuff like demon sightings and ghost hunting apps for their phones.

"Laugh if you want but at least the Council is trying

to protect our records and keep us out of the public eye," Tarren said.

"Is this the same Council that Charles was talking about today?" I asked. They all nodded, but I was still lost. "Who are they?"

Everyone turned to Helios. He sighed and wiped his hands clean before he spoke. "About fifty years ago, some high-powered paras . . ."

"Including Helios's ancient old grandfather, Hyperion, who flew in all the way from Mount Olympus," Tarren said.

"And boy were his arms tired," Avis added, then laughed himself silly while everyone else groaned.

Helios scowled at Tarren and Avis. "Hyperion is a Titan, not an Olympian. Haven't you read Rick Riordan?" Jeez, I thought as they stared at each other, they were taking themselves very seriously. But Helios looked away then continued his explanation. "They negotiated a deal with the state government to allow our kind to live a parallel life here as long as we don't use our powers."

"Your kind?" I asked.

"Paras," Tarren said impatiently.

"And by paras you mean . . . ?"

"Paranormal human beings, duh," she said.

"Including you," Helios added.

"Me?" I asked and nearly laughed.

"The whole para community," Helios said.

"There are more?" I asked.

Avis looked at me funny. "Did you think your family were the only ones?"

Before I could answer, Helios said, "Surely your parents told you about the Council."

I shook my head.

"Well, they should have," Tarren said. "Because if you mess up again, Josie Griffin, your family could be, you know, um, deposited."

"She means deported," Avis said. "To Saskatchewan."

"Your whole family can get kicked out of the country if you piss off this Council?" I asked, and they all nodded. Even if they were crazy, that hardly seemed right. "That's not fair."

"Fair?" Avis cackled. "It's separate but equal for paras and humans in the judicial system. Separate laws, separate courts, separate sentencing, all overseen by the Council."

I looked around Buffy's. At the girl with hoop earrings, sitting on a stool. The guy with blue streaks in his hair, messing with his iPod. The twins over by the door. Did everyone here think they were a paranormal human being? Or was it just Helios, Tarren, Avis, and Johann who were delusional? Or maybe they were trying to pull an elaborate prank on me? "So everybody here is a para? Even them?" I pointed to the gaggle of gaunt girls who were macking on Johann earlier.

"To tell you the truth, we're not sure what they are," Avis said.

"Obviously not entirely human," Tarren added.

"They followed Johann here one day, begging to be bitten," Helios said.

"They live near me." Johann looked annoyed, like an older brother who can't shake his little sisters.

"I think they're a coven who believe the kiss of death will keep them skinny forever," said Tarren.

"They are so tiresome," Johann said.

Tarren giggled. "Aren't you ever tempted, Yo? Just a little nibble?"

Johann waved his hand. "No, no. We don't do that anymore. Not the good ones, anyway. It's strictly animal blood these days." He sighed. "We're a dying breed."

"Except you're already dead," Tarren said and everyone, except Johann and me, laughed.

"Just what are you, exactly?" I asked Johann, because I wanted to see how far they would carry this.

"Isn't it obvious?" he asked and I shook my head.

"Vampire," he said as if it were no big deal. I tried to keep a straight face.

"And you?" I asked Tarren.

"A faerie, duh," she said.

I looked at Avis.

"Shape-shifter," he said.

"You mean like a werewolf?" I asked, and fought back a smile because he seemed like the least menacing person I'd ever met.

"What?" he asked, his mouth in a tight, angry line. "A brother can't be a werewolf?"

"No, no." I shook my head and held up my hands. "Far be it from me to say what you can and can't be. And you?" I turned to Helios. "Let me guess," I said. "You're the Greek god of the sun?"

He frowned at me. "Many generations removed, but technically, yes."

"And is everyone in this place also in anger management?" I asked.

"No," Tarren said. "Only the ones who get in trouble. Like us."

I couldn't decide whether to laugh or dive in and ask more questions. On the one hand, telling me they were vampires, werewolves, faeries, and Greek gods was capital *C* crazy, but on the other, it was fascinating. What would make a group of kids act like this? Boredom, drugs, too many bad novels and movies? Then again, they seemed so serious about it all.

"So?" Tarren said, staring at me with those intense green eyes. "What are you?"

I decided at that moment to go undercover because the truth was, I hadn't had this much fun in months but I knew if I was going to stick it out with them, I would have to play along. "I'm a . . ." I glanced from person to person. Avis crossed his arms and stared hard at me. Johann frowned while I hesitated. "Werepire," I blurted out.

"A werepire?" Tarren said, drawing back. "Sounds like a word I would say."

"It's a mix," I told her, as if I were offended. "My

mom's a shape-shifter and my dad's a vampire, so I'm a werepire."

They all looked at one another. "I've never heard of that," Tarren said.

"Can we interbreed?" Avis asked Johann.

"What powers do you have?" Helios asked me.

"None," I said. "Because of the cross-breeding. I'm like a mule."

"Ah," Helios said as if it all made sense now. "That's probably why your parents haven't told you about the Council. They probably thought it would never be an issue for you."

"Exactly," I said.

"And you really broke your boyfriend's windshield with an actual baseball bat?" Avis asked.

"You mean instead of sucking his blood or ripping his heart out with my claws?" I asked, enjoying myself immensely.

Suddenly Johann sat up and said, "Wait a moment. Vampires can't procreate."

"Don't you have parents?" I snapped.

"For societal purposes only," he said. "They did not birth me."

"Well," I said with a shrug. "I don't know what to tell you. My parents had me and . . . oh crapsicle!" I yelled and started digging in my pockets for my phone. "What time is it? I was supposed to be home for dinner at six."

"It's past six o'clock," Helios said.

"Crap!" I hopped up from the table. "I'm so sorry.

It's been great meeting you all." I checked every pocket on me and then realized that my phone must be in the khakis I left in the car. "But my mom is going to kill me. Not literally," I said and laughed a little. "Because werewolves don't kill their own children, right? Thanks for letting me join you!" I called over my shoulder as I hurried out the door.

chapter 6

running through the parking garage, I thought I heard footsteps behind me, but every time I turned around, I only saw shadows lurking. When I hit the street, the sun had started to set and the streetlights had come on. It was later than I'd thought and I knew that my parents would be livid. I ran all the way back to Illinois Street, glancing over my shoulder again and again because I couldn't shake the feeling that someone was following me. But the only person out was the homeless guy who'd made his bed of cardboard on a park bench across the street.

When I got to Gladys, I dove into the backseat. Sure enough, my phone was in the pocket of my khaki pants, but since New Josie didn't believe in planning ahead, the battery was dead and I was screwed. "Crap!" I yelled as I scrambled into the front again. I jabbed the key into the ignition and Gladys did her usual wheezing and barking, but she wouldn't turn over. "Come on, baby. Come on!" I pounded the steering wheel. I turned the ignition again and got the same sad response. "You can do it, Gladys. If there's ever a time I need you to go, it's now." I tried and tried and tried, but Gladys just wouldn't start. Defeated, I pounded my forehead against the steering wheel and yelled, "Crapitty crap crap!"

I jumped when someone knocked on my window. My first instinct was to scream and my second instinct was to pound my fist down on the door lock. I looked out the window, expecting to see the homeless guy, or worse, but instead I only saw a looming dark shape.

"Yosie?" I heard. "Are you alright?"

I cranked the window down—another advantage of having a crapmobile, the windows actually rolled down even if the car won't start. "Johann?" I asked, peering into the darkening night.

He stepped aside so light from the streetlight came into my car. "Are you having car troubles?"

"Uh, yeah, but what are you doing here?" I was really creeped out then. "Did you follow me?"

He leaned down and stuck his head in my window, but then he reared back. "What's that horrid smell? Has something died in your car?" He leaned forward again, sniffed, and licked his lips.

"No, it's just not very clean, but that's beside the point! What are you doing here?"

"I left after you. I live nearby. I heard you cursing in the car so I thought I'd see if you needed help," he said.

He stared into my eyes again. "Would you like my assistance?"

I snorted. "Johann," I said firmly. "Stop looking at me like that." I was about to roll up the window, but then I realized that other than finding a pay phone that worked or a public bus, I was out of options. I sighed. "Do you have a phone?"

Johann scoffed. "One of those pocket contraptions? Never! It's a crime what they cost. But you can come to my house and call from there."

Maybe I should have found the guy scary. After all, there was the whole delusional vampire thing to contend with, but at that moment my choices were to walk the deserted streets alone or go to Johann's house and call my mom. "How close do you live?" I asked.

"A few blocks," he said, pointing south. "In Lockerby."

It might not have been the smartest thing to do, but I got out of the car and walked with Johann anyway. There was just something about him that seemed utterly harmless and besides, if there was any neighborhood downtown that was safe and full of people, it would be Lockerby, so I figured I'd be okay. If he tried anything funny, I could run up on somebody's front porch screaming bloody murder.

But nothing happened. We walked silently through the quaint little streets, passing row after row of small wooden bungalows. I'd always loved this neighborhood because it looked like something out of a different time and a different place. The houses were small and packed tightly together, not like the gargantuan McMansions taking over the urban sprawl oozing from the borders of Indy. The whole area, with its white picket fences and blooming azalea bushes, was just so dang cute. I couldn't imagine anything bad ever happening there. And then I wondered if Johann was like me. Maybe he was bored with his sweet little life and pretending to be a vampire was his out, just like quitting the cheerleading squad and becoming an angry blogger was mine.

I followed Johann up the creaky front porch steps of his house. "After you," he said and held the screen door open for me.

The inside was nothing like I would have expected. Everything was straight out of an old home ec textbook. Totally *Leave It to Beaver*. The carpet was mint green. The couches were low and covered with plastic and the walls were covered with hideous paintings of big-eyed children lost in alleys. Weirdest of all was a giant stereo with an actual turntable and humongous speakers taking up one wall of the living room. Soft instrumental music, maybe a bossa nova, hummed along in the background. Johann stopped and held out his hand to me. Awkwardly I laid my hand on his icy palm. He tried to pull me close, but I kept my distance as he tugged me across the carpet, stepping in time to the music. "The telephone is in here," he said as he danced us through the living room and dining room, into the kitchen where I promptly wriggled away. God, he was wacko.

He flicked on a round fluorescent light to reveal orange and brown linoleum and a seriously old-school green fridge, like the one my grandparents had on their farm before they moved to assisted living in Florida. The phone was even more of a relic. It was mounted onto the wall and had a rotary dial. I couldn't hide my fascination.

"Whoa!" I picked up the clunky handset. "This thing is an antique!" I started dialing while I chuckled. "It's going to take me five minutes just to call my mom."

Johann leaned against the spotless yellow Formica counter. He looked tired and pale and I wondered if he could be sick. Maybe he had some horrible disease and pretending to be a vampire was part of his coping mechanism.

My mom picked up on the third ring. "Mom, I'm sorry, but it wasn't my fault," I said before she had a chance to get mad.

"My dad's coming to get me," I told Johann when I hung up. "But it'll take about fifteen minutes. We live in Broad Ripple," I explained.

"Do you mind if I have something?" He motioned to the fridge. "I'm famished."

"Go right ahead," I said and tried to suppress my grin. Guess vampires eat just like everybody else.

As he crossed the kitchen to open the fridge, his mother rounded the corner and we both jumped. I'm not sure who was more surprised, me or her. The way she looked from me to Johann and back to me, I got the feeling that Johann didn't bring home many girls. But I was too weirded out by her whole Donna Reed meets Morticia Addams vibe to say anything. The woman had a black bouffant hairdo with a tiny pink bow nesting on top of her head, which matched perfectly her crisp pink and white checked shirtwaist dress. And the weirdest part—she was actually wearing a little white apron tied in a neat bow around her waist. If it weren't for her pale skin and gray half-dead eyes, she would have looked like she just stepped out of a 1950s sitcom. No wonder Johann was so messed up.

"Johann?" she asked, her voice pitched an octave above any normal person. "Did you bring home a friend?" Then, I swear to god, she leaned forward and sniffed me!

I stumbled back until I was pressed against the countertop. Did I reek or something? Yes, my clothes had been festering in my gym bag for a few weeks in my backseat, but I couldn't possibly smell that bad.

"Hello, Elaine," Johann said from behind the refrigerator door. "This is Yosie."

Since good manners had been drilled into me since I was a toddler, I stuck out my hand and smiled politely. "Nice to meet you. I'm Josie," I said, exaggerating the *J*.

She reached for me shyly. When our hands met, I nearly jumped. She was freezing! Worse than my grandma who wore a cardigan even when it was eighty degrees outside.

I glanced back at Johann who had pulled out a white carton from the fridge and was getting a glass from the cupboard. "She's in my group and she had car trouble, so I told her she could use our telephone," he explained to his mom as he pushed back the edges of carton's spout.

His mother let go of my hand and continued to stare at me, perplexed. "But . . ." she said and paused. "Is she . . . ?"

"Huh?" Johann asked, distracted by the stubborn spout that wouldn't open. He glanced at her and then, sensing her discomfort, he shrugged. "She's half," he said. Then he looked at me. "What did you call it? Vamp-were?"

A surprised laugh popped out of my mouth. He was going to put on this show in front of his own mother! And she was going along with it? Wow. I pressed my lips together. "Werepire," I said, and the blood rushed into my cheeks because, no matter how much I might have changed recently, I still hated to lie to adults, an Old Josie trait I'd probably never lose.

His mother closed her eyes and inhaled deeply, then the tip of her tongue poked out and caressed her lips as she stood perfectly still two feet from me. Bizarre! I would never complain about my mom again.

"Her mom's a shape-shifter and dad's a vampire," Johann said, finally loosening the spout. "Did you ever hear of that before?"

His mother had closed her eyes and didn't seem to be listening, but still I sputtered, "Oh, well, I . . ."

embarrassed by how far this had gone. It was one thing for me to make up stuff to a group of weirdo kids I'd just met; it was another to lie to someone's mother, no matter how odd she might be.

Elaine opened her eyes. Her pupils had nearly overtaken her green irises and she rocked back and forth as she stared at me. I wondered if she might be crazy. Maybe Johann had some kind of hereditary mental illness. I turned to him because his mom was freaking me out. "You know . . ." I started to say but then I stopped when I saw him pouring what looked like dark, thick tomato juice out of the carton into his glass. The smell, though, was not tomatoey. It was something else vaguely familiar. A metallic scent that curdled my stomach. My mind reeled, trying to place that smell, trying to put it all together, the color, the consistency, the slight stench of raw meat lingering in the air.

Then it hit me. My head spun and my stomach squeezed. I tried to push the thought away but suddenly it all made sense and I couldn't deny it any longer. He was pouring blood into that glass. This was real. It was not a joke. Johann was a vampire. His mother was a vampire. And she wanted me for a snack!

chapter 7

i grabbed onto the counter to keep my balance as I inched my way toward the kitchen door. Mrs. Bloodsucker stood on the threshold, eyeing me suspiciously. I scanned the room for some way to defend myself, but I didn't know what I was up against. Was anything I'd heard and seen and read about vampires real? Did they have superhuman strength? Could they break my arm with one squeeze? Could they fly, turn into bats, and read my mind? Or had *I* lost my mind? Behind me, on the wall I saw a clock with a crucifix above the numbers. Jesus slumped against the cross. Was that a joke? Did they keep it for a laugh? Some sort of ironic pop art? Oh look, we're vampires and we have a cross in our house? Hardee-har-har. Who cared! Short of a silver stake, which I didn't happen to have in my pocket, I had no other chance for escape.

Just then Johann took a long swig of his bloody

drink. He winced. "Ugh, animal blood. Pig, cow, chicken, all mixed together, bleck! Just never the same as a fresh kill, you know?" He held the carton out to me. "Is this what your dad drinks?"

I saw the words *pasteurized* and *fresh* flash in front of me. For a minute I doubted myself. Was I imagining all of this? Was he really just drinking some kind of juice or was it milk and I'd gone nutty? Johann drained the last dregs from his glass. Then he wiped the back of his hand across his mouth and sighed. My fear must have been palpable because he cocked his head to the side and studied me for a moment. Then he glanced at his mother.

"Elaine!" he shouted. "Snap out of it!"

I whirled around in time to see her lips curling back, teeth exposed, a look of determination in her black flashing eyes. I ripped the clock off the wall and raised it above my head, ready to slam it into this vampire mama's chest, but Johann stepped between us. He grabbed Elaine by the shoulders and gave her a firm shake.

"I finally make a friend and this is how you act?" he shouted at her.

She crumpled to the side and whimpered. When she looked up again her eyes were gray, her mouth was pressed into a tight line, and she seemed contrite. "So sorry," she mumbled. "It's just that . . ."

Johann turned to me, shaking his head. "How mortifying. My apologies, Yosie. She doesn't get out much." Then he stopped. "What are you doing?" he asked, pointing to the clock held high above my head, the long white cord trailing to the wall socket.

I lowered it. "I, um, I was just . . ." I pulled it around in front of my face. "Will you look at the time? My dad is probably here, so I should, you know . . ." I set the Jesus clock gingerly back on the counter as Elaine shuffled out of the room. My heart pounded against my rib cage like a bird trying to escape, which was exactly what I needed to do. "I can show myself out," I said, stepping away from Johann and inching toward the dining room, trying not to make any sudden moves. All I had to do was get to the front door. Then I'd take off running down the street until I found my dad and I'd promise I would never do anything bad ever again because if this was what I had to deal with after bashing in Kevin's windshield, then it really wasn't worth it after all.

"What kind of host would I be if I didn't show you to the door?" Johann asked, looping his hand through the crook of my arm. I cringed away from him, afraid that he might want a little nip, but he seemed uninterested as he walked me back through the house, which was eerily quiet. "We aren't faeries, here. We do have manners!" He tossed his head back and laughed loudly.

"Why?" I asked, curiosity getting the better of me, despite how scared I felt. "Are faeries impolite?"

Johann rolled his eyes. "You did meet Tarren, didn't you? Dreadful manners I'm afraid. But what would one expect from woodland creatures?"

My heart had slowed down and by the time we

reached the porch I was beginning to question what just happened in the kitchen. Johann was so nice and calm. Maybe I'd misconstrued everything. We stood under the weak bulb attracting flitting moths. "Your mom . . ." I started to say.

A pained look crosses Johann's face. "Elaine?"

"She is your mother, right?"

"Well, you know how it is," he said but then he shook his head. "No, I suppose you don't because your parents are by birth. The rest of us, vampires anyway, form social bonds for show. Hasn't your father taught you anything about our culture?"

I stood silently. What could I say? That I'd been lying? Then what would happen? Would he get the munchies?

"I've heard of this in families that choose to pass. Don't worry," he said, patting me on the shoulder. "I can teach you everything. And look on the bright side"— he revealed a large gleaming smile—"maybe you will awaken your inner Dracula!" He tossed his head back and roared with laughter.

My dad pulled up to the curb. I'd never been so happy to see his gold Chrysler LeBaron in all my life. As I jumped down the steps and ran to the sidewalk, Johann called after me. "See you next week, Yosie?"

I didn't answer. I just kept on running.

Before my dad had a chance to roll out the we're-so-disappointed-in-you-Josie diatribe, I threw myself into the car and yelled, "Drive! Drive! Drive!"

"What? What's wrong?" Dad yelled back, but he slammed the car in gear and laid rubber on the street. "What happened?"

I turned around in my seat and watched out the back window, making sure there was no one following us. The street was quiet, except for a group of girls shuffling down the sidewalk into the shadows. "Oh thank god!" I sighed and flung myself forward. "I'm so glad you're here. I've had the creepiest night. Thank you so much for coming to get me."

Dad did a double take, looking concerned. "Are you all right?" he asked. "You seem really shaken up."

"Dad," I said, laying my head back against the seat, "I'm way out of my league. If you think playing home run derby on Kevin's windshield was bad, you should meet the kids in this anger management group." Suddenly I was laughing. It was all so unbelievable. I went back over the afternoon and evening in my head. Half of what I remembered couldn't actually be true, could it? All along I thought those kids were delusional, but maybe I was the one who'd lost my marbles.

"There's no one dangerous is there?" Dad asked.

This cracked me up even more. "I don't know," I admitted between hiccups of laughter. I'd laughed so hard that my stomach hurt and I felt nauseated and then it occurred to me that I might be laughing so that I wouldn't cry.

"It wouldn't surprise me," Dad said. "You know how these downtown kids are."

"Believe me," I told him. "You have no idea."

· · ·

When I got home, I immediately climbed in bed and logged on to JosieHatestheWorld on my laptop. Some of my blog friends had posted under the pix of me from earlier. SadSadie said, "Cute top!" and KKLaLa said, "Headbands are for a*holes!" Almost all of my readers were girls who'd been dumped. We were like a sad-sack sorority of heartbroken hellions. But truthfully, I was getting tired of all the whining about everybody's love life. What had started as a way for me to cry and moan about how Kevin and Madison had mistreated me had become a blabfest for my readers. *Oh, boo hoo, I got dumped, too! He has a new girlfriend and she's fat. I saw him the other night at Steak 'n Shake and I barfed up my French fries.*

Which was why I was so excited to have something new and interesting to post tonight. My fingers flew over the keys as I recounted what happened in group therapy and at Buffy's. As I typed, I tried to untangle all the knots in my mind and get every detail down, but I got stuck on what happened at Johann's house. No matter what I said, it didn't make sense. Finally, I typed:

I'm not sure what happened tonight in Lockerby. Is J's mother really a vampire or is there another explanation? Whatever the truth is, I'm going to have to find out!

I posted my entry but as soon as I reread the words, they seemed ridiculous. Who would believe what I wrote? Faeries, vampires, werewolves! No one would buy it. I didn't even really believe it and I was there.

I tried to think like a journalist. What would Graham Goren do if he was breaking a story? First, he'd do some research. I surfed the words *vampires* and *werewolves* and *faeries* on different search engines but all the usual stuff came up about books and movies and TV shows. How would you look up real monsters? Especially when Tarren said they kept their records off the Internet. I entered the words *Council* and *paranormal families*, which yielded nothing. I added *Saskatchewan* to my search because Avis mentioned something about it. A URL for a site called ParaHunt came up, but the link was broken when I clicked it.

Then I remembered a stupid listserv Kevin and some of his d-bag friends were part of called demon hunters. I typed it in and the site came up complete with melodramatic music and overdone fonts. Lists of weapons, supposed sightings, ghost-hunting phone apps, and pix from "hunts" populated the pages.

When Kevin was into it, I thought the info on the site was bogus. Just a bunch of crap for jackweeds in leather jackets who liked going on fake occult chases to amuse their tiny minds. Now I wondered if the supposed demon hunters were on to something. Even if they were, which was worse? People like Kevin who wanted to hunt down supposed demons, or the kids I hung out with today? Definitely the idiots hunting demons were worse because the kids I met weren't out to hurt anybody. In fact, they were some of the least judgmental, most accepting people I'd ever been around. Much nicer than the stupid cheerleaders I used to count as friends.

I felt kind of bad about the post I had written. I probably sounded like I was making fun of the paras, which wasn't my intention. Then again, it was a great story and would probably get more traffic to my site. I could always change it later if I wanted. Besides, I was exhausted from such a crazy day. I decided to sleep on it then reread what I'd written in the morning. I closed my laptop and let my eyes drift shut. Only depressed girls with boy problems would read what I wrote, so I didn't have to worry anyway. Besides I didn't use anyone's name, only initials.

As I lay there, something dawned on me. Despite how bizarre my day had been and how genuinely scared I was at Johann's house, I felt happier than I'd been in months. Instead of Kevin and Madison staring at me from behind my eyelids, I thought of Tarren with her flaming red hair buzzing with excitement as she struggled to tell the story of the guy in the alley. The bizarre way she tripped over words. And I remembered Avis falling off the chair, which made me chuckle. Who ever heard of a clumsy werewolf? Then I saw Helios inviting me to go to Buffy's. Beautiful, perfect Helios. Greek god was right.

chapter 8

Later that week, Sharon Osbourne pointed to the toilets. "Scrub brushes and cleaner are in the cabinet."

Surely, I was in Hell. How else to explain a woman who looked exactly like Ozzy's wife telling me and another girl to scrub toilets? Oh right, this was my community service.

"Any rubber gloves?" I asked, swallowing hard to keep my Nachos Grande down.

Mrs. Osbourne's double glared at me. "No, there aren't any rubber gloves. What do you think this is? Buckingham Palace?" she yelled over her shoulder as she stomped out of the bathroom.

I glanced at my cleaning partner and said, "You mean this squat cement block building on the south side of Indianapolis isn't a sprawling British castle?"

She gave me a warning glance and jerked her head toward the door.

"Keep your comments to yourself!" Mrs. Osbourne reappeared then added, "And don't use too much cleaner. One squirt per commode. Put some elbow grease into it." She disappeared into the hallway again.

Sighing, I trudged to the cabinet for a toilet brush. "Never thought I'd be reduced to a toilet scrubber." I handed the other girl a brush and a bottle of Mr. Clean.

She pushed her long blonde hair away from her face and I could see that she was pretty in that fresh farm girl kind of way with freckles across her nose and thick hair so shiny she must drink gallons of milk or something. "Have you seen Ozzy?" she whispered. "Because I think his wife is looking for him."

My mouth fell open then spread into a huge smile. "Duuuuuude," I whispered. "I know! Weird, right?"

"So weird," she whispered. "And you want to know what's weirder?"

"What?"

She stepped closer to me. "Her name is actually Maron."

I guffawed, loud and stupid. "Shut up."

"For reals. I've been calling her Sharon Osbourne in my head for a week now."

"That's awesome," I said, then I stuck out my hand. "I'm Josie."

"Kayla," she said. "But I think I'm going to skip shaking your toilet brush hand."

I laughed and wiped my hand on the back of my

cutoffs. "Good idea. Have you done this before?" I asked, studying my brush.

"I'm a toilet virgin," she declared.

"Me, too!" I lifted my brush like a soldier. "Let's do this thing." I used the bristly end to push open a stall door. The hinge squeaked and I cringed, expecting Armageddon of the Butt. When I stepped inside, I was surprised. "It's not so bad," I told Kayla as I squeezed Mr. Clean into the bowl. Just to be spiteful, I gave it an extra squirt. "Guess girls aren't such slobs, but if we were working at a guys' shelter . . ."

"Hey!" Maron Osbourne shouted from the hall. Kayla and I both popped out of the stalls and saw her glaring at us from the doorway again only this time she had a girl who looked about twelve with her. "Stop your gabbing and get back to work!" she yelled. "What do you think this is, Dunkin' Donuts?"

So help me Lord, I couldn't stop myself. "I'll take two glazed and a coffee," I said.

Kayla ducked her head but I could hear her muffled snorts beside me.

Maron crossed her arms over her ample chest. I swore her dyed hair was going to burst into flames as she glared at me with those witchy eyes. "Kayla," she barked, and Kayla jumped. "Come with me. I have a job for you and Sadie."

Kayla handed me her toilet brush along with a look of pity then she scurried across the floor. The other girl, Sadie, clung to Kayla's arm like a frightened toddler, but who could blame her with Maron-Sharon running the show. "And you," Mrs. Osbourne said to me, "can finish cleaning the bathrooms on your own."

After they were gone, I pulled my phone out of my pocket and took a picture of myself with two toilet brushes. At least that would be good for a laugh on my blog.

When my first three-hour shift was over (and all the toilet bowls sparkled) I looked for Maron Osbourne to sign my official community-service time sheet. I found her at the receptionist desk, under the HELPING AMERICAN GIRLS sign, reading the *National Enquirer*.

"My aunt JoJo loves that magazine," I told her as I slid my time sheet across the desk. Of course, JoJo and I read the *Enquirer* to laugh ourselves silly, but I got the feeling Maron might have read it for real by the way she narrowed her eyes at me.

"They break a lot of stories no one else has the guts to report," she told me.

"I want to be an investigative reporter," I said, leaning on the desk.

She raised one eyebrow.

"Really. I'm trying to get into University of Chicago to study journalism."

The other eyebrow went up and Maron leaned forward to stare at me. "I think Ms. Babineaux sent me the wrong kind of girl."

I stood up straight. "What's that supposed to mean?"

"It means, I don't need your attitude here, missy."

I stepped back. "What attitude?"

"That one," she said.

"I don't have an attitude," I assured her. "I just want to finish my community service before the school year starts, then I can get on with my life. So if you'll just sign my time sheet . . ."

Maron picked up a pen but she didn't sign. "Listen, I don't need some rich, entitled spoiled brat to come in here and get nibby."

"Jeez," I whined, kind of hurt by her baseless accusations. "I'm not spoiled. My parents are teachers. I made a mistake once. Now I'm paying for it."

She pointed the pen at me. "You come in here, do your work, and leave. Got it? You're not here to make friends with these girls. You're not here to save them. Keep your nose out of everybody's business, or I'll make sure Ms. Babineaux reassigns you. And let me tell you, picking up trash on the side of the road with a bunch of sex offenders won't be a cake walk like scrubbing toilets."

"God," I said. "Fine."

I could see a little smirk on Maron's maroon lips as she scrawled her name across my time sheet. I grabbed it from her and headed for the lounge where my bag was in a locker by a bank of beat-up old computers.

I muttered to myself about what a bee-yatch Maron was because I thought I was alone until I walked past one of the faded couches and saw Kayla laying down reading a battered copy of *Pride and Prejudice and Zombies.*

"Hey," I said. "That's one of my favorite books."

She slammed the book closed and sat up. "Are you joking?"

"No, why would that be a joke?" I asked her.

She bit the side of her lip and shrugged. "Guess it wouldn't. It's just that, most people make fun of me for reading."

"Most people are idiots," I said.

Kayla smiled. "For a rich entitled brat, you sure are good at scrubbing toilets."

"Are you making fun of me now?" I asked, hand on my hip.

She laughed. "What'd you do to set Ozzy's wife off like that? She ripped you a new one."

"I know, right?" I said, rolling my eyes. "She must have it in for me."

"Watch out or she'll send you a box of poo," Kayla said, and we both snickered then looked over our shoulders to make sure Maron wasn't behind us with a set of brass knuckles.

"You're not an actual HAG, are you?" Kayla asked.

"A hag?" I asked. "I'd hope not!"

She pointed to the sign on the wall. "Didn't you notice? Helping. American. Girls."

I swallowed a giggle. "Oh my god. It is HAG."

"That's what the girls who live here call ourselves," she explained.

"Nice," I said. "Can I be an honorary HAG? I am court ordered to be here. Community service for the screwup."

"Well," Kayla said, considering. "I'd have to teach you the secret handshake and . . ."

We were interrupted by Maron who bustled into the lounge carrying an overstuffed backpack dripping clothes and shoes from its exploding sides. "Hey you!" she yelled, pointing straight at me. "Your shift is over."

"Sorry," I said stepping away from Kayla who quickly ducked down on the couch and stuck her face into her book. "I was just . . ."

"You were just leaving," Maron told me, and I agreed. She pushed through the back door and I caught a glimpse of her opening the Dumpster before the door slammed closed.

"That was Rhonda's stuff," Kayla said quietly. "Maron made me and Sadie get it all together."

"Who's Rhonda?" I asked.

"Another HAG," Kayla said. Worry crossed her brow. "She's the second girl to disappear since I've been here."

I shrugged. "It *is* a place for runaways, isn't it?"

Kayla scowled at me. "Yeah, but Rhonda was just getting herself together. She signed up for GED classes and got a part-time job at 7-Eleven then things started to get weird with her." She looked around nervously.

"You guys were good friends?" I asked.

She nodded. "It doesn't make any sense. Why would she leave without her stuff?"

"I don't know, maybe she just . . ." I trailed off because I had no explanation.

Kayla looked up sharply. "She was scared."

"Of what?" I asked.

Kayla drew in a breath as if she was going to explain something but then she thought better of it. She shook her head and looked away.

"I'm sorry your friend took off," I said. "Look, um . . ." I dug around in my bag for a pen and paper and scribbled my cell number. "I could lend you *Sense and Sensibility and Sea Monsters*, if you want." I handed her the paper. "It's a good read and . . ."

A loud pounding shook the back door. "Open the door!" Maron yelled. "I got locked out."

Kayla and I looked at each other and cracked up. "Should I leave her out there?" Kayla asked. "Let the lunatics take over the asylum?"

"She'd just come in through the front," I said.

"I'm not sure she's that smart," Kayla said. "But I probably shouldn't wait to find out, which means you should get out of here." She smiled down at the contact info I gave her and placed it carefully between two pages of her book. "Thanks for this."

"Sure thing," I called as I ran for the front entrance. "See you next week!"

chapter 9

When I stepped into the late afternoon humidity, I hesitated before heading to my car. Something didn't add up here. Kayla was right. It would be strange for one of the girls to take off and leave her stuff. And even stranger that Maron wouldn't keep shoes and clothes in case another runaway showed up without any luggage. Plus the whole thing seemed to freak Kayla out and that bothered me. These girls might be runaways, but that didn't mean their lives were disposable. I probably should have left right then, but I had that feeling like someone was being wronged and I didn't want to walk away from injustice. So against my better judgment, I slipped around to the back of HAG to see exactly what Maron had thrown away.

I found the big green Dumpster by the back door and just as I was about to lift the lid, I heard the door open. Quickly I slid between the Dumpster and a brick wall because if Maron caught me snooping she'd have me spearing trash on the side of the road in a nano-second. Note to self: never hide behind a Dumpster on a sweltering August day again. Three words: stink, stank, stunk!

However, crouching back there gave me a perfect view of who was walking out of HAG—none other than Atonia Babineaux, my social worker, which seemed kind of odd. She had her phone pressed to her ear. "I'll be there in five minutes," she said as she walked by. She hung up and practically skipped across the pavement. Her skin was rosy, her hair was soft and silky, and she looked vibrant. A far cry from the withered old woman I met in her office the other day. Either she really hated her social work job or the lighting in her building was truly evil. As she passed the Dumpster, I heard a cell phone ring. I expected to hear her pick up, but instead, she stopped and turned around and I panicked. Was it mine? I squished my bag against my body to muffle the noise, because it would be mighty hard to explain to my social worker what the heck I was doing behind a Dumpster. Then I realized it wasn't my ringtone. It didn't seem to be hers either because she walked toward the Dumpster with a quizzical look on her face. I pushed myself farther against the wall but luckily, instead of coming around to the side, where she could have seen me, Ms. Babineaux stepped in front. I heard squeaking metal as she lifted the lid and the ringing got louder. Obviously it was coming from inside the trash bin. Who would throw away a perfectly good cell phone? Ms. Babineaux must have been wondering the same thing because she stood there, muttering, "What the . . . ?" until the ringing stopped and the phone beeped twice as if it had gotten a voice message. The Dumpster rattled as the lid crashed down.

Ms. Babineaux huffed, then stomped off, growling, "I don't have time for this." I stayed hidden until I heard a car door slam and an engine start. I peered out and saw her pull away in a gray Prius. I slid out from behind the Dumpster, my heart still revving like the Indy pace car. I could almost feel the bacteria from my gross hiding place crawling over my skin and entering every bodily orifice. Would Graham Goren hide behind a Dumpster for a story? Probably. Even if he ended up with hantavirus and Ebola and stank like fourteen-day-old cabbage and sweaty jockey shorts. I heard the phone ring again. I was about to lift the lid to find it when Maron's loud barking voice came through the back door.

"Fine! Fine!" she shouted. "I'll take care of it."

I made a mad dash out of there.

As I was running back to Gladys, I realized why Tarren said it wasn't fair that she lived down here while Helios lived on the posh north side. I could tell that the hood used to be a nice place, like a hundred years ago, because the houses were huge and the yards were bigger. But between the abandoned buildings, weed-choked lots, and the run-down Victorians, there wasn't much else to see. Least of all people. You'd think the whole place had been deserted. I slowed down and caught my breath.

When I rounded the corner toward my car I saw a group of guys my age hanging out in front of a fried chicken joint. They looked harmless enough, jacking around with one another, but still, there should be a law against males between the ages of fifteen and twenty-five hanging out in groups of more than three. Put a bunch of girls together and we'll combine our brainpower to make us smarter (and meaner, as I found out first hand). But if you put a group of guys together, they drain each other's brain capacity straight into their pants and start thinking with their wieners, especially if a girl in shorts walked by. I considered crossing the street, but Gladys was only half a block past these jokers, so I'd have to cross the street, walk down half a block, and cross back, which would be weird. I decided to duck my head and plow past them quickly. Plus I could see some people hanging out on a front porch down the street. Surely these guys wouldn't act too stupid.

Or not.

"Hey, baby," one of them said as soon as I got near them.

I kept walking, head down, car keys ready in my pocket.

"I said, hey, baby." A tall, lanky guy blocked my path. I could see his red boxers hanging out of his low-riding jean shorts and he had his Colts hat on cockeyed so only one lazy brown eye with a silver hoop above the brow was visible.

"Excuse me," I said firmly then I tried to step around, but he sidestepped and stayed in front of me as if he were guarding me on a basketball court. "I never seen you around here." The other guys snorted like the pigs that they were. "You live nearby? Maybe we could hang out."

"No, thanks," I said and stepped the other way, but he was quick and got in front of me before I could pass him. I stopped and put my hands on my hips. Most idiots back down the minute you confront them so I said, "I'm trying to get by."

He held up his hands and shrugged. "And I'm trying to get with you."

"Not going to happen," I said, staying calm, but inside my stomach squeezed and my heartbeat quickened. It was only a short ride from this feeling to being spitting mad. I tried to breathe deeply like Charles demonstrated during group therapy so I wouldn't do something I'd regret. "I'm on my way to meet my boyfriend," I lied and tried to step around him again.

This time he reached out and pushed my shoulder. "He don't have to know, baby." The other guys behind us whooped and slapped each other five.

I stepped back, furious now. The only way I could get around the jerk was to walk into the street, but then I would be farther away from my car.

"I'm Drey," he said, stepping closer. "What's your

name, babe?" Then he ran his grubby fingers across the belly of my T-shirt and I lost it.

There was a part of my brain that knew I was about to make the wrong choice, but that part got pushed out of the way by the other part that wanted to kick this a-hole in the balls. I knocked his hand away and shouted, "I am not your babe! Now get out of my way!"

"Oooh," one of the guys behind me said. "A live one. She'd be fun on her back, Drey."

With his chest out and arms bent, Drey towered over me. He shoved his face down in mine. "Why you gotta be so unfriendly?" A drop of his spit landed on my cheek. I could see the fury in his eyes and even though I was pissed, I was also scared. All I had to do was make it to my car and get the door open, but I had no idea how I'd get past him. Before I could figure out what to do, I heard another voice.

"Hey," she said. "Back off, Drey!" Everyone, including me, turned to see a tiny girl storming up the sidewalk, red hair flying like a wild fire.

"Tarren!" I yelled, stepping around the giant jerk-face in my path.

She stopped in her tracks. "Josie?"

"It's me!" I ran to her side.

She put her hands on her hips and looked up at Drey. "Why are you always harassing my friends, huh?"

"Tare, baby. You don't gotta get so mad. I didn't know she was a friend of yours," Drey said.

"And what if she wasn't?" Tarren demanded. "Why would you be bothering her anyway? Poor girl, just walking down the street and you act like a pam dig."

I see a couple of the guys try not to laugh at Tarren's mistake.

"Aw, come on now," Drey said. "Don't get all psycho on me. I was just having a little fun, you know. Wasn't gonna hurt her or nothing. Right, girlie?" he asked me.

"You scared me half to death," I told him from behind Tarren.

"Drey?" Tarren said, her voice a low warning.

"What?" he asked, Mr. Innocent refusing to admit he was wrong.

"Apologize!"

"I ain't apologizing for nothing!" He shook his head, but I could tell he was half thinking about it anyway.

"Come on, man," one of Drey's posse said. "You know how Tarren gets when she's mad. Junk's going to start flying around and pretty soon you'll be lifting your leg to pee on that tree." The other guys laughed, but it was a nervous kind of chuckle that had them all shifting from foot to foot, watching the showdown between tiny Tarren and the big galoot.

I was fascinated. What would she do? Would I get to see her in action? Could she zap him like she claimed at therapy? I didn't believe her then, but after what happened at Johann's house, I thought anything might be possible.

"I don't want you mad at me, baby," Drey said

before Tarren had to pull out some badass faerie moves. "I thought we was blood."

She softened a little, relaxing her hands and smiling. "Sure, sure," she told him. "We're blood. But my blood can't be macking on my friends. And Josie here . . ." She pulled me to her side. "She's my girl."

Even though I was still pissed off at Drey, I took a deep breath and tried to regroup, thinking maybe I could salvage the situation if I was calm. Then, even though it sort of killed me, I stuck out my hand and I said, "Hey, Drey. I didn't know you were a friend of Tarren's. How about if we call a truce?"

"Yeah, well," he mumbled. "Why you walking around in this hood by yourself anyway? Don't you know it's dangerous?" But then he held out his fist for a knuckle bump, which I gave him, awkward as it was.

Tarren turned to me and said, "What are you doing in this dump? I thought you lived in Rod Bripple." She stopped and thought about this then tried again. "Dod Bripple? No wait, don't tell me, I can get it." She stopped, took a breath then said, "Broad Ripple!"

I nodded, relieved that a) no one laughed at her and b) she found the word before I had to correct her. "Community service." I pointed toward HAG.

"Right. Come on." She turned away from the guys who'd absorbed Drey back into their huddle but then she looked over her shoulder. "See you around. And remember"—she pointed to her own eyes and then to him—"I've got heads in the back of my eyes." I elbowed her and shook my head. "I mean, eyes in the back of my head," she yelled. Then she turned to me and said, "That guy never learns."

Tarren led me to a huge, ramshackle Victorian house painted twenty different colors with a wrap-around porch, crazy turrets, balconies, and intricate gingerbread trim all around the eaves. The front yard was a riot of wildflowers and butterflies. We climbed the crooked steps to the porch where five people in gauzy, flowing clothes lounged in various states of repose across wicker couches, hammocks, and big pillows strewn all over the place. I saw more people on blankets in the side yard.

"Do all these people live here?" I asked.

"Spriggans, no. This is the result of good old haerie fospitility."

"Hairy what?" I asked.

She raised an eyebrow. "Hostility? No that's not it. Hos-pi-ti-li-ty . . ."

"Hospitality?" I asked.

"Yeah, that's it! Faerie hospitality. We can't say no if someone asks to stay with us. Literally. We are incapable of saying no." Tarren picked up a pitcher of what looked like lemonade from a little rickety table and poured a big glass. "You want something to drink?"

"I should really be going . . ." I started to say, but Tarren picked up the glass and handed it to me. I took a sip of the sweet, cold nectar because I was parched and I didn't want to be rude. As soon as it hit my stomach, the core of my body melted and I was so relaxed that the thought of leaving seemed ludicrous.

Tarren smiled at me. "What's your hurry, honey?"

"No hurry at all," I said and took another gulp of the shimmering liquid.

Tarren draped herself over a gold silk chaise lounge beside the table. She patted the cushion for me to sit, which I did.

"This is the most amazing thing I've ever tasted," I told her and continued to drink. "What is it?"

"Ambrosia," she purred, as she reached for the pitcher then she laughed. "No, that would be what Helios drinks, right?" She poured me another tall one. "Sorry if I stepped on your toes back there."

"What? Are you kidding? You totally saved my butt." I took the drink from her but before I sipped it, I looked her straight in the eye. "Why are those guys so afraid of you?"

She lifted her shoulder coyly. "You know why."

I took the leap. If Johann's mom was real, then Johann was real. And if Johann was real, then Tarren was, too. "But do they know?"

"Humans, ugh!" she said with a dismissive wave of her small pale hand. "They're so boring after a while, don't you think? Anything I do, they just explain away as some strange coincidence or force of nature. They think they're so smart but really they're blind to ninety percent of what goes on in the universe. Bee-prains."

I sat up straight, ignoring her garbled expression

because I was ready to defend my species, but then I remembered, Tarren thought I was one of her kind.

"Anyway why didn't you take care of Drey yourself?" Tarren asked.

"Remember?" I said. "No powers."

Tarren slung her arm around my shoulder and leaned close to my face. "Darling, we really must unleash your inner demon!"

"Demon!" I said, pulling away.

Tarren giggled and sipped her glass of the yummiest drink ever. "What? You don't consider shape-shifters and vampires demons?"

I hesitated. "Avis and Johann seem like nice guys."

Tarren nodded. "They are. I mean, Johann's annoying and all, but he's not evil."

I leaned in close. "His mother tried to take a bite out of me."

Tarren smacked my thigh. "Get out! Couldn't she sense you were one of hers?"

This caught me off guard. "I suppose the werewolf in me threw her off?" I said, but it came out like a question.

Tarren nodded. "Makes sense."

"Anyway Johann stopped her," I said, and then it hit me. Today was the second time someone from my group kept me safe. I might not have known what they were, but it was clear, they weren't going to hurt me. I studied Tarren for a moment. She was so small that I could probably have wrapped my hands around her waist. "You guys really watch out for one another, don't you?"

"Yes," she said. "We do." Then she lifted her glass. "And now," she said, clinking hers against mine, "you're one of us."

Slowly I raised the cup to my lips and took a long drink which filled my body with a warm, happy buzzing. "Seriously," I said. "What's in this stuff?"

"Flutterby milk," Tarren said then laughed. "I mean, butterfly milk."

"And how do you milk a butterfly?" I asked, half joking.

"Like this," she said and without taking her eyes off me, she reached up and snagged a blue-winged critter flapping by. "First you catch it." She brought the bug close to her mouth. "Then you ask for its forgiveness." She whispered something near its soft, fluttering wings. "Then . . ." She snapped her fingers closed. I cringed, not wanting to see the mess in her hand as she opened her fingers one by one, but in the center of her palm was a little pool of shimmering liquid. "You turn it into the essence of itself." She tipped her hand and poured the milky stuff into my glass.

I stared at my cup, not sure what to do.

"It might sound funny," Tarren told me. "But that's kind of what I think our group is."

I stared at her, uncertain. "The group is a smashed-up butterfly?"

"No," she said. "It's a place to find your essence. We can't let the world define us. We have to be true to what's inside us no matter what some stupid Council says we can and can't do." She reached out and tapped her finger against my sternum. "What's inside there, Josie Griffin?"

"I . . . I . . . " I stammered because the truth was, ever since Kevin and my two best friends betrayed me, I'd been trying to find my center again.

"You should come back to group," she said.

"What makes you think I'm not coming back?" I asked, embarrassed that my reticence about the group might have been obvious.

"You seemed pretty weirded out by everything. And after you ran away from us at Buffy's we weren't sure we'd ever see you again. You are coming back this week, aren't you?"

I looked into my glass and thought about my essence. Who was the real Josie? And could this group help me find her? I lifted the glass to my lips. It was still delicious. "I'll be back," I told her.

"Good," she said and gave me a quick wink. "It'll be nice to have another girl around."

chapter 10

I nearly attacked my laptop when I got home because I was dying to post about how little Tarren saved me from Drey the douche. I didn't think anybody would comment on the post I'd made the night before, but I was wrong. PissyGrrl said, "Are the guys in your group cute?" Sadie said, "Have you done a drive by of Madison's house lately?" And BitterBrit wrote, "Is there group therapy for people who get dumped?" I couldn't believe it. They'd completely missed the point. They were so caught up in their own drama they barely noticed what I posted. Only KKLaLa, as usual, had something interesting to say. "Zowie!" she wrote. "Those freaks in your group are weirder than my friends. And talk about a nightmare family! J's mom makes mine look almost normal. Maybe you could sic the freaks on Kevie Boy. They could rip his heart out like he did yours."

I chuckled at the thought of Kevin, who fancied

himself an amateur demon hunter, being hunted by the paras and I posted a reply to her comment, "I wish! I'd love to be able to hex his butt!" Then I spent the next ten minutes writing a post about my first day of scrubbing toilets at HAG (complete with the photo I snapped), hiding from Atonia, and being rescued by Tarren.

Just as I was finishing, I got a text.

Sorry to bum u out 2day . . . overactive imagination :)
And I was sad that Rhonda went AWOL. Can I still borrow
Sense and Sensibility and Sea Monsters? Thnx KKLaLa

When I saw her signature, I did a double take. How many KKLaLas could there be in the world? I quickly texted her back.

R U the KKLaLa who reads JosieHatestheWorld?

A minute later her response came back.

OMG!!!! U R that Josie! Just read your post about HAG!

For reals u read my blog?

For reals u write that blog? Everybody at HAG loves it!
U R a freakin' celebrity!

I leaned back in my chair and cracked up. I couldn't believe the girl I'd scrubbed toilets with was the same girl who been posting comments on my blog. Although when I thought about it, it made sense. I remembered from her earlier posts that she had a preggie scare a month ago and her parents kicked her out then her jerkwad boyfriend dumped her when it turned out she wasn't pregnant. My heart broke for the girl I'd met earlier that day. I had no idea what a mess her life was.

Another message popped up from her.

Did u rly hear a phone in the dumpster?

YES! Weird, huh?

Rhonda's maybe?

Gazoinks! She could be right and that would be seriously suspicious because who would take off without her phone? Quickly I texted back.

Go outside and call her. See if it rings in the dumpster.

After curfew. Can't leave but I'm sooooo worried!

Do u want to call the police?

No! R was underaged. If the police find her, they'll send her back home, which is worse than being here. R loved reading yr blog. Called herself Rebound. B4 she came

here, she ran away and lived with her boyfriend, but then
he kicked her out bc he had a new baby mama—jerk! Her
heart was broken in a 1000 pieces. Now she's gone. I feel
so helpless.

I lost my breath for a moment. I remembered Rebound's posts. She was always so sweet and thoughtful. Telling other girls to hang in there and to be strong.

We have to find out if it's hers! Make an excuse to leave.

I CAN'T! If Maron catches me, she'd kick me out.

After what happened to me with Drey earlier, my stomach churned at the thought of any girl roaming around that neighborhood. I couldn't take it! It was so unfair. I had to do something.

Give me her cell #. I'll be there in 20 mins to check it out.

U R awesome! Digits below. Gotta go. Mrs. Osbourne is on the loose.

I ran downstairs and grabbed my keys. "I'm heading out!" I told my parents as I hurried through the kitchen.

Mom looked up from the eggplant she was chopping. "I don't think so."

"But I have to help a friend," I pleaded.

Mom's knife stopped and Dad peered over the top of his newspaper at me. "One of your friends?" Mom asked, then they looked at each other with hope in their eyes and I sensed that my eternal grounding might end early if I played my cards right.

"Who?" Mom asked.

"Nobody you know. It's somebody new I met at my community service."

Mom smiled at me hopefully. "Is she nice?"

"Yeah," I said, playing along. "You'd really like her." Mom and Dad looked at one another again, doing that kind of silent parental exchange where you're sure they can read each other's minds. I was hoping they were thinking that making new friends was better for me than sitting in my room alone.

"I promise I won't be gone long," I said.

My dad nodded and said, "Take your time."

"But call if you're going to be out late," Mom told me.

"Thanks. Love you!" I ran out the door before they could change their minds.

I was kind of nervous to go back to the Southside, but I figured as long as I stayed parked close to HAG, I should be fine. Indy felt different as I drove, though. The straight streets now seemed slightly sinister. What was hidden behind all those big, leafy oak and elm trees? Who was lurking in the darkness of the parks? How many families like Johann's and the others had slipped into seemingly normal lives behind the shutters and the doors on all these ordinary houses? Even those annoying Zombie Apparel billboards seemed creepier than stupid all of a sudden.

My world had been so small until this week. I used to blame that on being from a sleepy city smacked down in the middle of corn and bean fields. Now I knew I was seeing only a little bit of what was real. And what I used to think were enormous problems (my friends betraying me, my boyfriend cheating on me) shrunk in comparison to what people like Kayla and Rhonda and my para friends dealt with every day. At least I had a place to live with parents who cared and there was no weird Council threatening to uproot us if I messed up again. I felt a glimmer of Old Josie wanting to come out, but this time it wasn't so bad. It was the part of me that liked to help people who were getting the raw end of the deal. Like the work I did for Habitat or the other fund-raisers I used to get all stupid excited about. Only helping someone personally, like Kayla or Rhonda, felt even better than baking cupcakes for some cause I couldn't see.

When I got to HAG, I killed my lights and parked in a dark alley behind the building. My old friends and I used to do dumb crap at night like toilet paper an opposing team's goalposts before a game. Or stake out the houses of guys we liked. We thought we were so awesome, all cramming into a car, cranking the music, and acting like idiots. Even though I didn't want to act like that ever again, I did wish someone was with me, like

Tarren, because getting out of the car alone was freaking me out.

But I promised Kayla I would help her, so I opened the door and ran on tiptoe across the lot to the gray Prius parked under a security light. I crouched behind the car, straining my eyes and ears to make sure nobody was around. The only thing I heard was the buzz of air conditioners and the beating of my heart. I dashed toward the Dumpster. From my old familiar hiding place by the wall, I opened my phone and punched in a text to Kayla.

Here now. Calling R.

I dialed Rhonda's number then I waited.
And I waited.
And I waited some more.
What the hoo-haw! Did she give me the wrong number? My legs started to cramp. I texted Kayla again.

Did u give me the right number?

A second later my phone beeped, which made me jump and gasp. Some undercover reporter I'd make! Kayla wrote back.

Yes! Did u call it? Did it ring?

I dialed Rhonda again and waited, straining my ears this time, in case the phone got buried under more trash, but still I heard nothing. Which couldn't be right. I peeked out from my hiding place. No one was around so I sneaked to the front of the Dumpster and slowly opened the lid. It squeaked like a rusty old coffin in a horror movie and the stench that wafted up was worse than zombie breath. I hit redial and listened to the phone ring in my ear, but nothing happened in the Dumpster.

"This can't be right," I mumbled to myself. I must have been doing something wrong. I dialed Kayla's number so we could talk.

"Josie?" she whispered when she answered. "I'm not supposed to talk on my cell inside."

"Are you sure you gave me Rhonda's cell number?" I whispered back.

"Of course I am," she whisper yelled. "Can't you hear it?"

"No. I've called it over and over and nothing's happening." My whispers bounced around the inside of the Dumpster and filled up the murky alley. "It just keeps going to her voice mail. Maybe the battery died." I stuck my head farther inside the Dumpster until my shirt pressed against the disgusting greasy edge and my face was inches from a reeking bag of garbage. "It has to be in here!" I said, but just as I was about to start digging through bags, I heard a familiar bark through Kayla's phone that made me jump.

"Hey, you! You know you can't use that phone in here."

"I was just, I . . . I . . ." Kayla stuttered.

"Give me that!" Maron yelled.

"No, please," Kayla said, then the phone went dead.

I dropped the lid, which crashed down and echoed through the alley. Certain Maron heard, I ran as fast as I could to Gladys, praying all the way that my car would start.

chapter 11

all weekend, I was dying to know what happened at HAG after Gladys laid rubber and squealed away faster than a speeding turtle. I tried a million times to reach Kayla Saturday and Sunday, but she never answered. I was freaking out because what if Maron stuffed her in the Dumpster? Or what if Kayla was pissed at me and didn't want to answer? Finally, when I got out of bed on Monday, there was a text from her.

OMG! I thought Maron was going to KILL me on Fri, for reals. I told her u were my cuz calling b/c my grandma is sick. Boo-hoo! Maron is no dum-dum, tho. She threatened to call my parents! I begged her not to. Told her my dad is bad news. She took cell and computer privies for the wknd. Ha-ha! Thanks for your help. Wish I knew where Rhonda went :(

...

I was relieved, but still, I felt bad. I was sure that had been Rhonda's phone in the Dumpster. What else could it have been? As much as I wanted to go back to HAG to find out more, I couldn't. Gladys was going to the doctor to find out what was causing the terrible clanking under her hood, so I was bus bait for the day. And anyway if I showed up at HAG on my day off, I'd get canned, then I'd never find out what happened. The best thing was to bide my time until my next shift when I could see Kayla again. Plus I had to get ready for anger management.

I changed my clothes at least 65,000 times. What would a werepire wear? I tried a red mini, striped tank top, and flip-flops. Then I put on black from head to toe. With every outfit, Helios floated through my mind. Would he like a skirt, shorts, or pants? Maybe a skort with leggings? A better question would be, why should I care? I threw all the clothes in a pile on my unmade bed and scowled at myself in the mirror. I swore when Kevin and I broke up that I would never again try to impress a guy. "Old Josie cared what guys thought," I told my reflection. Then New Josie marched to her closet, closed her eyes, and pulled out the first two things she felt—vintage black and green plaid men's golf shorts and a pink Hello Kitty tee on which I'd drawn a mustache and a bull's-eye target. Perfect.

...

When I got to therapy, everyone was there but Charles, which meant there was an open seat beside Helios (where Charles sat last time) or the seat where I sat last time. I paused in the doorway and did the quick mental math. If I chose the seat I took last time, I was afraid it would seem like I didn't want to sit by Helios, which I did. But if I took the seat by Helios, would it seem like I had a thing for him? Which I might, but I wasn't sure I wanted everyone to think that quite yet. But wouldn't it seem like I was blowing him off if I purposefully didn't take the seat beside him? Then again, everybody else was in the exact same spot as last week, so maybe I should sit in mine, too. Then I thought nothing could be more boring than dissecting every single detail that goes through a girl's mind when it's infatuated with a paranormal hottie.

I walked across the room. Helios looked up at me, smiled, and pointed to the seat next to him with his eyebrows up. I plunked down beside him with a huge dorkball smile on my face and he leaned toward me. I melted in his warm glow. "I wasn't sure you'd come back," he said.

"It's this or juvie," I told him.

"I feel your pain," he said.

I turned in my chair and tried to ignore the blush crawling up my cheeks. Then I saw Johann, staring at me from across the room. His eyes were dark and cold.

His mouth a tight, straight line. I stared right back at him. "What?"

"You don't even say hello, Yosie?" Johann complained.

"Hello," I said.

He leaned forward and grinned. "Hello," he replied in a deep, husky voice like we were in a dark, smoky club with disco balls and hookahs. I rolled my eyes, which made Tarren laugh.

She smacked him on the shoulder. "Lay off, Yo," she told him. "Your mind tricks don't work on her."

"Must be the vampire in her," Avis said. "Makes her immune."

"That's all," I told Johann with a smile. I didn't want him to know that he was a cut-rate vampire with no mind control powers because he was a good guy, even if he was a 100 percent cheese ball who liked to partner dance.

Charles ambled into the room with a mess of folders in his arms. He looked momentarily confused by the new seating arrangement, but then he dumped his stuff on the empty desk and said, "Why don't we get started. Helios, we haven't heard from you for a while. Tell us about your week."

"Uneventful," Helios said.

Charles pressed his fingers into a tent in front of his mouth. "The last time you shared, you spoke about the tension between you and your father."

"He returned to Greece," said Helios, as unemotional as marble.

"Yes, but he'll visit again and the same issues will be there," Charles said.

Helios's nostrils flared. "Perhaps," he said. "But my life is none of his affair."

A cloud passed by the sun outside and the room momentarily darkened. Helios rolled his eyes and grimaced.

"What do the rest of you think about that?" Charles asked. "Do your parents have a say in your life choices?"

"Depends on whether they care enough," said Tarren, glumly. Avis reached out and laid a hand on her slumped shoulder.

"How about you, Josie? What role do your parents play in your life?" Charles asked.

"When I was little they had a say in everything I did, but now, it's less than they'd like but more than I want," I said.

Charles chuckled. "Well put," he said. "Asserting oneself as an individual separate from the parents is a long, slow process. Maybe the longest for you, Johann, because you've been, what, eighteen since the 1980s?"

"Dang!" I blurted out. "Being stuck in high school for thirty years straight would make me want to be homeschooled!" Everybody laughed, even Johann. But I wasn't trying to be funny and I had a million questions about Johann's family after the other night. I leaned forward. "Did your mother or father, you know, change you?" I asked. The hairs on the back of my neck prickled as I waited for his answer.

"No, no, I was created outside an East Berlin discotheque in 1982 by an ancient one. Transylvanian actually," Johann said, looking directly at me, as if I should be impressed. *Oooh, Dracula.* "I've been with Augustus and Elaine for the past twenty years," he continued. "But it's not so bad. Except when Elaine tries to mother me. I suppose she misses her own children."

"And how do you feel when she does this?" Charles asked.

"It's entirely embarrassing and exasperating!" Johann said. "Like when Yosie was at my house the other night . . ."

Everyone turned and stared at me. I shrank in my seat and glanced at Helios who watched me with one eyebrow raised. "My car broke down," I offered meekly. "I needed to use his phone."

"And Elaine immediately pounced on her," Johann continued.

"Literally," I muttered.

"She should meet my mother," Helios said, and my heart did a little flip. "The minute I bring anyone in the door, Mother is all over her with a thousand questions."

This time I stared at him, wondering how many girls he brought home every week. Mr. Paranormal Romance himself!

"What about you, Avis?" Charles asked.

Avis smiled apologetically. "What can I say? I've got it good. My parents give me space when I need it but they're also always there for me. I think shape-shifters

111

are like that. They get that everybody needs a little room to change. Is that how your mom is, Josie?"

I thought about this, then I said, "Yes. My mom gives me space, even when she doesn't understand me." Tarren scowled at me, which was weird because I thought we had a moment on her porch the other day. But I knew that kind of look. It was the same one I used to get in the halls at school from a group of girls who didn't make the cheerleading squad. They were nice as pie to my face but when they thought I wasn't looking, they stared daggers. I looked away from Tarren. Why was it so hard to be friends with girls, even faerie princesses? I just hoped Tarren's powers didn't make her super pissy!

Charles spent the next forty minutes yack-yack-yacking about how we could get along better with our parents. I spent most of that time stealing glances at Helios's amazing profile. He had possibly the most exquisite nose I'd ever seen and I had the overwhelming urge to draw pictures of him or sculpt him to capture that perfection. Every once in a while, he caught me looking at him and we locked eyes then I got all hot and bothered and had to squirm in my seat like a three-year-old who needed to pee.

Outside, after the session, we all gathered on the sidewalk. It was a gorgeous end-of-summer evening. The humidity had lifted and there was a breeze in the air that promised fall would soon come. Every day felt a little shorter than the last, and that evening the sky was already pinkish as the sun considered its descent.

"Buffy's?" Tarren asked.

"Nah," said Avis. "It's too nice to go underground." He rocked his foot back and forth on his skateboard like he was itching to ride.

"Anyone feel like some b-ball?" Helios asked, miming a jump shot.

"Now that's an idea," said Avis. "You got a ball?"

Helios nodded. "In my car."

"Ladies?" Avis asked, turning to us.

"I'd go," I said, because once again, what else could I possibly have to do?

"Fine," said Tarren. "But I'm playing, too. You can't leave me out just because I'm a girl and I'm short."

"We let Johann play," Avis said.

"Very funny," Johann said. "You believe because I am a ballroom dancer, I am not a man, well let me tell you, I am more of a man in my small finger than you are in your pants."

"What?" Avis laughed. "You want to put your finger in my pants? That's nasty!"

"Op, nope, erp," Johann protested. "That is not . . ."

"In or out?" Avis asked.

"In," Johann said, defeated.

The courts in the park by White River were deserted. "I swear," I said, climbing on top of a picnic table, "sometimes it's like a nuclear warhead landed on Indy and everyone's either dead or hiding in a bomb shelter."

"I love it when no one's around," Avis said. He jogged onto the court and held out his hands for the ball. Helios bounce passed it to him and ran lazily toward the basket. Avis passed it back to Helios who missed an easy layup.

Tarren dropped her bag on the table beside me. "You're playing, aren't you?"

"I'm not so good at ball sports," I admitted.

Tarren rolled her eyes and pointed to the court where Johann ran around, flapping his arms like a spaz. "Believe me, there's not much competition here. Everyone kind of sucks."

"All right," I said. "As long as I'm not totally embarrassing myself."

As we passed the ball around and tried to hit the basket, Tarren asked, "Can you believe the incredible BS Charles spouts sometimes? I mean, was he serious about those 'Tips for Getting Along with Your Parents'?"

"My favorite was, 'Don't use sarcasm,'" I said, dribbling the ball then bouncing it to Johann who missed it. "The next time I'm in a fight with my dad, I'll be sure to try that," I said as sarcastically as possible.

"What about, 'Use *I* statements, not *you* statements'?" Avis asked. He stole the ball from Johann and tried to bounce it between his legs, but ended up hitting the side of his ankle and sent the ball rolling across the court. Helios jogged over to get it.

"Does '*I* think *you* are annoying, Mom!' count?" Tarren asked.

"What I find infuriating," Helios said, as he double dribbled back toward us, "is this false message about celebrating yourself for who you are when in the next breath we are reminded of the retribution from the Council if we so much as dare to reveal our true natures." He planted his feet and tried a two-pointer from the top of the key. The ball hit the rim and ricocheted to the side.

"Word, Bolden Goy!" Tarren said, then she stopped, looked at Avis and they both laughed.

"What's that, baby, a non-Jew with lots of chutzpah?" he asked.

"I meant Golden Boy," she said, still laughing. She held up her hand for a high five from Helios, but he stared angrily at the basket he just missed.

Johann retrieved the ball and stood on the free throw line. He cradled it near his belly then heaved it up in an underhand pitch. The ball soared past the basket and over the backboard. "Airball!" I yelled. Tarren wasn't kidding. These guys really did suck. I got the ball and ran a wide circle to the right, evading Helios who tried to smack it away from me. I stopped, planted my feet, and aimed. By some miracle of physics, my ball swooshed through the net. Before I could stop myself, I was jumping and hollering. I did a toe-touch then pumped my fist in the air and yelled, "Go, Josie, go!"

Everybody stopped moving to stare at me. Tarren held the ball against her hip. "What the heck was that?"

"Sorry," I muttered, my face blazing in embarrassment.

"Hell to the no," Avis said. "You're a cheerleader?"

"Was! Not anymore," I told them, but I laughed because it was all so ridiculous. Like the cheerleader in me was the para in them just waiting to pop out! They continued to stare at me and Helios seemed almost miffed. "What?" I said. "None of you do any sports or anything at school?"

"We're not allowed," Helios said.

That stopped me cold. "You mean the Council?"

"Wouldn't be fair, now would it?" Tarren bounced the ball by her side. "How could the poor little human boys and girls compete with us and all our superpowers?" she said in a whiny baby talk voice. Then she looked around and seeing that no one but we were in the park, she took the ball and zoomed around the court. She was so fast, her purple T-shirt and gossamer green skirt were a blur in the fading sunlight. She zipped by me, swooshing my hair to the left, then circled Avis twice before she leapt, one leg bent, the other straight behind her, the ball held high above her head. She floated like a little leaf toward the basket where she deposited the ball gently through the hoop. She alighted, for just a moment, on top of the back board, one leg in an arabesque, then she hopped and landed softly beside me. "Where's my cheer?" she asked.

"Dang!" I yelled, smacking myself on the forehead. "That was crazy beautiful. Did you guys see that?" I looked at Johann. "What can you do?"

He shifted from foot to foot. "Uh, well, this is not my sport," he said. "I'm better at swimming."

"You know, the whole not having to breathe thing?" Tarren pointed out.

"And I like ballroom dancing, too," he said and did a quick little two-step turn.

"So I gathered," I said.

Helios stepped forward. Behind him, the sun had become a fiery orange ball, slowly sinking over the river. He picked up the basketball and jogged to center of the court. As we all looked around to make sure no one had come into the park, the court lights flickered on. Helios stood in the center of their glow. He took a breath and then threw the ball down. It bounced high into the graying sky. I lost sight of it among the gauzy purple clouds. Helios bounded across the court then leapt into the air. I watched him soar up and over our heads, nearly in slow motion, twisting and turning, seeming to pause in mid-air as he struck position after position. He was a bird. He was a shooting star. He stood at the helm of his chariot, the golden orb of sun trailing behind him. Then, he spread his arms and legs as if they were beams of light and he flipped head over heels, before he snagged the ball, fell back toward earth, and glided to the basket. He slammed down the ball, but it caught the rim and shot off to the left, sending Helios careening to the side. He tucked into a little ball and smacked the pavement hard, then rolled to a stop at the base of the goalpost. We all ran toward him, calling his name.

I got there first and dropped down to my knees. "Are you all right?!" I yelled, reaching toward him. But he looked up at me with fire in his eyes. I reared back.

He stood, blood dripping down the side of his face, and yelled in Greek. I'm not sure what he was saying, but I got the idea. He lifted his fists over head and cursed the sky then suddenly a loud *POP!* resounded through the night and the lights shut off.

"Oh come on, Helios!" Tarren said from somewhere in the dark.

"Every time you get mad, dawg, you bust up the lights," Avis said.

"By the wings of Hermes!" Helios cried. "I can't help it. It pisses me off when I miss."

"Holy crap!" I laughed in disbelief. "That was awesome."

I heard Tarren giggle. "It was pretty funny."

Our eyes began to adjust. We found ourselves in a circle beneath the basket.

"Before you missed," Johann said, "it was a very daring move."

"Is your head okay?" I reached for Helios, but he flinched away from my touch.

"Yes, of course," he said, and in the dim light I could see that the blood was gone and his skin was perfectly intact.

"Whoa," I said, stepping back. "You already healed."

"Try explaining that to the school nurse," Tarren said. "Rule number 725. We're not allowed to do anything that might cause energy, I mean, injury, in front of the student body."

I shook my head. "I'm sorry, you guys. I didn't realize there was so much you weren't allowed to do."

From down the block we heard the rumble of a car engine. Johann, Tarren, Avis, and Helios huddled a little closer to one another as a black car slowly cruised past the basketball courts.

"What's wrong?" I asked.

"Shhh." Avis pulled me closer to the group. We stood stock still as the car idled for a moment on the street in front of us, then someone shone a bright flashlight toward the courts.

"Just be cool," Avis told everyone.

The light skimmed over us and I felt Helios, who was directly behind me, shudder. Then the car squealed around the corner. As it passed under a streetlight I saw *Impala* flash from the rear bumper and my stomach dropped. "What the heck?" I said, wondering if it had been Kevin. Was he following me?

"Do you think it's the DH?" Tarren asked Avis.

He shook his head but he looked a little worried. "Probably not."

"What's the DH?" I asked.

"Dip heads," Tarren said.

"Douche hats," Avis added.

"Dumb hicks," Helios said.

"No, really, who are they?" I asked.

"Just some idiot self-appointed demon hunters," Avis said. That sent a shiver through my body. Then Avis broke the awkward silence with one of his weird crowing guffaws. "But they missed the best part of the show!"

Everybody laughed, but nobody seemed all that amused.

"Do they do that a lot?" I asked.

"It's sort of random," Tarren explained. "They're out looking for trouble, so if we ignore them and act normal, they move on."

"Anybody want to head over to Buffy's?" Avis asked.

"Sure, I'll go," said Tarren.

"Me, too," said Johann.

"Can't," I said, digging my phone out of my pocket to check the time. "I'm bus bait tonight and the next one leaves in fifteen minutes."

Helios brushed little flecks of asphalt off his clothes. I noticed his hands were shaking. Probably from the hard fall he had taken. "I'm heading your way, Josie. I can give you a ride, if you want."

"Really?" I tried to wipe the big, goofy grin off my face and appear nonchalant. "I mean, if it's not a big deal or anything."

"No problem," he told me with an equally uninterested shrug.

"All right, then we'll catch you later," Avis said as he followed Tarren and Johann off the court.

"Will you be okay?" I called after them, thinking about that car and who might be driving it.

"We can take care of ourselves," Tarren called.

She was right. I had no need to worry about them. If

anyone, especially someone as stupid as Kevin and his posse, messed with my para friends, they'd regret it and that brought a little smile to my face.

"My car is a few blocks away in a private lot," Helios said. I followed him into the darkening night.

chapter 12

When we got to Helios's car, my mouth fell open. "That's your ride?" I asked, pointing to the crazy beautiful sparkling gold car with shiny hubcaps and dark tinted windows.

"Yes, it's an Infiniti M hybrid." Helios ducked his head and bit the side of his lip. "Not my first choice."

"Dang, man," I said, slowly walking around the rolling curves of its fender. "What was your first choice then? A Rolls-Royce?"

"I'd rather have something a little less"—he opened the door for me—"ostentatious."

The new car smell enveloped me as I slid onto the soft gold leather seat. "Then why did you get it?"

"My father," he said from the driver's seat. "You know, the whole golden chariot thing." He pressed a button and the dashboard lit up, but no sound came from the engine. "He just can't let go."

All I could do was laugh.

"After I wrecked my Mercedes, I asked him to get me something simpler and this is what he came up with," Helios told me as we silently glided out of the garage.

"How'd you wreck the Mercedes?"

We pulled onto Meridian Street. He drove with one hand on the wheel, the other poised on the console between us. I could feel the warmth emanating from his bronzed skin. "A fight with my father, a little too much nectar of the gods, and a race with the setting sun. We think we're in charge of our destinies. That we won't make the same mistakes as our fathers and our father's father, but . . ." he trailed off and sighed. "In the end, it's all so passé."

After seeing him get mad on the basketball court, I could only imagine what that fight was like. "Is that why you're in the group?"

"Sort of. I was supposed to lose my license." He grimaced. "That wasn't the first time I had a car problem. I tend to speed," he confessed, eyebrows up. "My mother pulled a few strings and got me into the group instead."

"We should have a side support group for people with car issues," I joked. "Auto Anger Management."

"You smash them and I crash them," he said with a grin.

I watched the trees, buildings, and billboards whiz by the window as I laughed. "This baby has speed," I said, patting the dashboard. "I'm lucky to get Gladys up to sixty-five. And then she rattles like a skeleton on a roller coaster."

Helios slowed down and took a ramp to I-465, the highway that circled the city. "I haven't opened her up yet," he said as we merged into traffic. The streetlights spilled into the car and I noticed that Helios's face glowed. He looked at me and smiled. It was the first time I'd seen him look genuinely happy and it sent shivers up and down my back. The left lane was open. I felt like we could merge onto a moonbeam and drive straight to the large yellow moon slowly rising in the east. "Want to see how fast it'll go?" he asked, but he didn't wait for an answer.

As the car rocketed forward, I fell back into the cradle of my seat. We zipped past the other cars, which looked like tired dogs meandering down a country lane. I reached for the dashboard. "Helios!" I said, but I was laughing. "You're going to get busted."

"Relax," he told me. He was more at ease here than I'd ever seen him. His shoulders were down, his mouth was soft, and his eyes sparkled. We hugged a curve to the left and my whole body leaned toward him from the centrifugal force. I caught sight of the speedometer, which read eighty-five miles per hour.

"Seriously," I told him. "If you get a ticket . . ."

He turned toward me. Our faces were inches apart and the moon swathed us in its glow. "But doesn't it feel good?" He nearly hummed.

"Yes," I said, melting in his gaze. The number on the dash crept toward ninety and my heart inched up toward my throat. "But you have to slow down."

"Is that really what you want?" he asked, but I couldn't answer. He straightened out the wheel and released his foot from the gas. "Sorry, I didn't mean to scare you."

"You didn't." I rearranged myself in my seat. "I thought it was a blast. But if you got caught . . ."

"Ah, yes. Realizing the consequences. The key to managing my anger." He shook his head. "The only problem being that my kind are not known for controlling their impulses. Look at my ancestors. Warring and fighting. Trapping one another. Creating monsters to stir up trouble. All the way back to Zeus. That guy is a complete megalomaniac!"

As soon as the words left his mouth a heavy cloud passed over the moon and a flash of heat lightning brightened the sky. Helios rolled his eyes and shook his fist, then yelled, "Oh whatever!" He muttered, "I can never get a freakin' break." He turned to me. "The whole all-knowing, all-seeing thing gets old so fast."

I laughed and shook my head as he crossed three lanes and exited from the highway. We stopped at a red light on the surface street under a looming Zombie Apparel billboard. The girls stared down at us like scarecrows in halter tops and micro-miniskirts. "Do you like those ads?" I asked, pointing up at the Zombie Love Attack!

Helios craned his neck to see then he shook his head. "They look like those girls who follow Johann around," he said. "All skinny and weird. Hollow-eyed and kind of stupid. I like girls with a little more spunk and a little more meat on their bones." He looked me up and down and grinned. "Like you."

I wasn't sure whether to be flattered or not. "Uh, thanks, I think."

The light turned green, but we didn't move because Helios had turned in his seat to stare at me. "That was a compliment," he assured me.

I was liquid. A little puddle sloshing around in the seat. My head fell to the side and my mouth went limp. My lips tingled and all I wanted to do was kiss him. But, just as I tilted toward him, my phone beeped. I jumped, breaking the spell between us. Helios exhaled and leaned away. The stoplight turned yellow and Helios gunned it.

As we moved through the intersection, I scrambled to get my beeping phone out of my bag. "Sorry, sorry, sorry," I muttered. "I don't even want to answer it. Somebody's texting me. Which is totally weird. Nobody texts me anymore," I rambled on, embarrassed and disappointed. I opened the phone and saw a message from Kayla—

Need your help! Sadie's gone. Freaking out. I'm next!

"Oh my god," I mumbled, thinking of tiny little Sadie out on the streets alone. I immediately texted back—

Where R U?

"Everything okay?" Helios asked.

"I don't know." My phone beeped again.

@ HAG. Hiding in the bathroom. Pls help.
They're coming 4 me.

I texted back, WHO? because I had no idea what she was talking about. Her parents, maybe, or her ex-boyfriend. Then, I looked up. "Where are we?" I asked Helios.

"On the west side. Sorry for the detour. I'll take you home."

"No, wait." I turned and leaned on the console between us. "I know this is kind of weird, but I have a friend who needs me to pick her up."

He glanced at me, eyebrows flexed.

"She's on the south side. Near Tarren's house." Kayla hadn't texted back so while I talked, I punched in the words, B there soon! then I hit SEND.

He frowned. "I don't want to go all the way back downtown. Tell her to call someone else."

"Seriously?" I ask, surprised by how cold he's gone all of the sudden. "But she doesn't have anyone else. Look, it's a long story," I pleaded. "It's just that, she's one of the girls where I'm doing my community service and something's wrong. Girls keep disappearing and now she's worried."

The relaxed and happy speeding Helios was gone. Now that stony mask he wore during group therapy was back in place. "Why is it any of your concern?"

"Because," I said, then I hesitated. "She's my friend."

Helios frowned. "You've only been working there for a week, Josie."

"But I've known these girls longer than that. I have a blog and. . . ." I shook my head impatiently. I didn't have time to explain empathy to Mr. Greek God. "I need to go there. If you can't help me, then just drop me off here."

Helios scoffed. "And then what? You'll take the bus?"

"Maybe. I don't know!" I looked out the window, searching for a way to get to Kayla.

"You shouldn't wander around the Southside at night alone," he told me.

"No kidding, Sherlock," I muttered. "But I can't ignore her. She asked me for help." We stopped at a red light. I looked at him and pleaded with my eyes. "Come on, Helios. What else have you got to do?"

"Play Wii," he said drily.

I punched him on the shoulder. "This will be much more interesting, I promise."

"How, exactly, will this be interesting?"

I grinned at him. "Speeding isn't the only way to get a thrill. How about sneaking a girl out of a shelter. Sounds fun, doesn't it?"

"No," he said. "What if I get caught?"

"You didn't get caught speeding," I pointed out.

He closed his eyes and sighed. The light turned green and the person behind us honked. "I don't like putting myself in harm's way," he said, and I laughed. "What?" he demanded.

"Some Greek god you are!" I said.

That seemed to touch a nerve because he immediately did a U-turn and headed south.

"So you'll do it?" I asked.

He gripped the wheel with both hands and focused on the road. "That depends on what we're doing exactly." He glanced at me again. "You do have a plan, don't you?"

I thought about this. What was I going to do? How could I sneak Kayla out of HAG? And then what? It wasn't like I could take her home with me. Or even if I could, that didn't change that other girls at HAG were missing. And of course, there was the problem of how I was going to either get in to HAG or get Kayla out. "Well," I said, biting my lip. "How good are you at acting?"

Helios shrugged. "Greeks know their tragedies."

"Good," I said as I texted my plan to Kayla. "Because you're going to be Kayla's cousin from southern Indiana."

chapter 13

nothing could be more out of place than Helios's
sparkling gold car parked right in front of sucky old HAG,
except, of course, Helios himself striding in through the
smudgy front door of the building. I wished I could see
what happened inside. I bet Maron did a giant double take
then tugged her shirt down to expose yet more cleavage
when he walked in. And the girls probably swarmed him
like bees to ice cream, but who could blame them? I was
hoping Kayla got my text and played along with the story
of her "cousin" coming to get her so she could visit her
ailing grandmother in the hospital.

I watched the door from behind Helios's tinted windows, then looked at the clock on the dashboard, then
watched the door, then looked at the clock. Five minutes
passed. How could it be taking this long? Had something gone wrong? Should I call Helios? Or text Kayla?
Or burst inside wielding a bat then drag my friends out

before Maron had them both cleaning toilets for eternity? Ten minutes went by and I was ready to drive the car through the front door, but I knew I had to control myself. Then, just as I was about to explode from impatience and worry, the HAG door swung open. Helios had his arm looped through the crook of Kayla's elbow as if they'd known each other forever, but both of them looked a little shaky and uncertain as they hurried toward the car.

As soon as Kayla slid across the backseat, she reached up and wrapped her arms around my neck. "Oh my god! Oh my god!" she moaned. She had me in a death grip. "You're such a genius and a lifesaver. How did you ever think of having a gorgeous guy pose as my cousin?! It was brilliant."

"Kayla," I croaked and squirmed. "Let go. You're hurting me!"

She gave me one final squeeze then she fell back against the seat. "Thank you. Thank you. Thank you for rescuing me."

I rubbed my neck, wondering what had gotten into her. This was more than just freaked out—this was terrified.

Helios slid into the driver's side. A trickle of sweat ran down the side of his face, which was uncharacteristically pale. "Easy as baklava," he said, but there was the slightest quiver in his voice. As if the Sun God's hard-as-marble composure had cracked a bit.

Before I could ask if he'd been nervous, Kayla shot

forward, grabbed for me, and began shouting, "Go! Go! Go! Maron and that creepy lady are coming outside!" She banged the back of the seat.

Helios jammed the car into gear and squealed away from the curb. I turned to see Maron and Atonia under a streetlight, pointing at the car. "Holy crap!" I ducked down, head below the window's edge. "Do you think they saw me?"

Helios sped around the corner. "No way," he said, checking and rechecking the rearview mirror. "Nobody can see through these windows. They're way too dark." He looked at me. "Right? They are dark, aren't they? There's no way they could have seen us."

I inched my way back up again. "I hope to the high heavens not. That creepy lady was my social worker."

We hit the highway and Helios floored it. Once we were moving, he took a deep breath and wiped a hand across his brow. "Whew! Glad that's over." He reached over to pat my knee. "Don't worry. I'm sure she didn't see you." He seemed almost as shaken up as I was and let his hand linger on my thigh as if to comfort both of us.

My heart was still racing and I wanted to intertwine my fingers with his while I took deep breaths to calm down, but Kayla stuck her head between us. "Wow, you two are criminal masterminds. Helios just strode in there like he owned the place and told Maron that I had to leave with him right away. Like it was a matter of life and death because our poor sick granny was going to croak any second. I didn't even have time to get my stuff together," she said. "I just grabbed his arm and headed for the door."

"But what happened earlier today?" I asked. "Where did Sadie go? Who's coming after you? And why were you so freaked out when you texted me?"

Kayla slumped in the backseat, thin and pale. "Oh, Josie," she said with tears rimming her tired eyes. "You'll think I'm crazy if I tell you."

I glanced at Helios who lifted one eyebrow. "Believe me, Kayla," I said. "I've heard all kinds of weird stuff lately that you couldn't even hope to top. Just tell me what happened."

She took a deep breath. "Sadie was really freaked out. Something spooked her after Rhonda left. She kept saying that the devil was after her, but she's from a really religious family down in southern Indiana so I thought she was one of those crazy Bible kids, you know, who take all that stuff way too seriously. She stopped eating, though, and she was getting real, real skinny. I kept telling her that she had to eat, but she said she couldn't."

"Maybe she was anorexic," I said.

Kayla bit her lip. "I don't think so. At least she wasn't a week ago. That girl could put down mad ice cream."

"Bulimic?" I guessed.

"I think she was just too scared to eat," Kayla said. "She told me it was going to happen. She warned me. She said, 'The evil one is coming for me.' She begged me to sleep in the bunk with her, but of course I didn't." She buried her face in her hands.

133

Helios glanced at me and asked quietly, "Did you know any of this?"

I shook my head. It was all news to me.

Kayal continued to moan, "I should have done what she asked, because this morning . . ." She looked up, horrified. "She was gone."

"Why didn't you tell me this sooner?" I asked.

Kayla fought back tears. "I just met you and I wanted to be friends. I was afraid if I laid all of that on you, you would think I was insane and wouldn't want to hang out. But when Sadie went missing, I didn't know who else to call. You're the only person who's been nice to me in so long."

"It's okay." I reached over the back of the seat and held her hand. "I'm going to help you."

"Thank you." She squeezed my fingers. "It's been the same with the other girls who disappeared, Bethany and Rhonda. Every one of them got scared and skinny then they were gone but they left all their stuff behind."

"That part doesn't make any sense," I said, half to myself and half to Helios.

"It's after me now," Kayla announced.

"What is?" I asked.

"It's like I'm dreaming, or at least, at first I thought I was. I mean, what else could it be?" She looked lost as she tried to explain. "Whenever I fall asleep. Like today when I was reading on my bunk. It came into the room. I could feel it. Smell it. Hear it creeping. But I couldn't move. I couldn't wake up. It was there, though. I know it. And I felt it. It climbed on top of me."

I sucked in a deep breath and Helios shot me a worried look. Oh crap, I thought. Was there a perv on the loose? Was someone abusing the girls?

"It weighed a million pounds and just sat there, perched like a giant evil cat." Kayla pressed her hands into her chest. Her eyes were wide and haunted. "And I could feel it, draining me. Taking something from me. Sucking the life out of me."

I let a long, slow breath go. Maybe Helios was right. Maybe I didn't know Kayla very well and she was a kook. Then again, that's what I thought about the paras at first.

"Sounds like a Vrachnas," Helios said under his breath.

"A what?" I asked.

"That's what we call them in Greece, anyway. It's a kind of demon who comes when people are sleeping." He was very matter-of-fact and hardly bothered by what he was saying. "She sits on your chest and smothers you."

My mouth dropped open. "Are you making this up?"

He looked at me like he was annoyed. "Why would I do that?"

I leaned in close to him and whispered, "You mean you believe this?"

He chuckled. "Oh right, sorry. Forgot. Human on board." He turned to Kayla and gave her a sympathetic smile. Then he spoke to her in a loud, slow voice as if she were a small child or a dotty foreigner. "It was probably just a common condition called sleep paralysis. It happens to some people when they're under a lot of stress. You can't breathe, you can't move, you imagine or dream something is trying to kill you. It's a part of REM sleep. I wouldn't worry about it." He glanced at me and winked like we were both pulling one over on the dumb humans to keep them from flipping out.

"No," Kayla said. She looked up with those haunted eyes. "It was real. That's how it started with Rhonda and Sadie. They thought they dreamed it. Then they got weaker and weaker every time they went to sleep until they were gone. And I was next."

All right, I thought to myself. *You've got your vampires. You've got your werewolves. You've got your faeries and Greek gods. So why wouldn't there be soul-sucking demons running a shelter for runaway girls? And how unjust would that be?* At that moment, I didn't know what to think but I decided that I believed Kayla and that I had to help her no matter how scary the whole thing might be. "What are we going to do?" I asked Helios.

"We?" he said.

"Yes!" I said, and it hit me. "We! The paras. We have to help the girls. Let's go to Buffy's and find the others."

Helios looked over his shoulder. "She can't go to Buffy's," he whispered.

"You guys took me there," I said.

"Yeah, but you're a . . . you know."

"Right." I sat back and tried to think of another plan.

"Then again," he said with a shrug, "southwestern cheddar poppers sound pretty good right now."

"I'm sure it'll be fine," I said.

He leaned in close and whispered, "Anyway if she sees or hears anything she shouldn't, Tarren can just zap her."

Avis and Tarren pushed me into a corner of Buffy's and let it rip.

"Are you out of your frickin' frackin' freakin' skull?" Tarren was up in my face, almost spitting. "What the hell were you thinking bringing a human here?"

"And where did you find her?" Avis asked, his head bobbing and arms flapping. "What if she tells other people? Do you know how much danger you're putting us all in?"

"First off," I said, pressing my hands against their shoulders to back them up a little. "There are other non-paras here." I pointed to the love zombies huddled around a table like junkies over a trash can fire. "And secondly, Kayla needs our help." I looked over at our table where Helios chowed on a big basket of cheddar poppers and chicken wings while Johann loomed over Kayla, salivating. "Oh crap," I muttered. "That's not good."

Tarren glanced over at them then rolled her eyes. "What did you expect? You brought him fresh meat. Muman heat, I mean, human meat! Blonde female human meat, you idiot."

"Something about that girl's got him all revved up," Avis said.

Tarren turned back to me and balled up her fist. "I should hex you into . . ."

"Just wait!" I pleaded.

Helios sauntered over gnawing on a half-eaten Buffalo wing. "I've never seen Johann this bad over a chick before." Then he gave a little half-amused snort.

Tarren exploded. "You think this is funny?"

Helios shrugged. "Yeah, kind of. He's talking like some Gothic romance dude about fate and destiny and lost love and how she smells just like Wiener schnitzel and sauerkraut and how he wants to take her dancing in East Berlin. He's totally into her."

"Seriously?" Tarren said, hands on hips as if she was slightly offended by the idea of Kayla getting this much male attention. "I've seen mannequins with more personality than that girl."

"She's not usually like that," I said. "Something happened to her at HAG. That's what I'm trying to tell you."

We all looked over in time to see Johann run his fingers through Kayla's long blonde hair. He almost trembled as the strands fell behind her shoulder. Then he trailed his finger down the side of her pale neck where a faint blue vein pulsed. "Oh crap!" Avis said and we all ran for the table.

I climbed over the back of the booth and pushed my way between Johann and Kayla, which wasn't easy because Johann wouldn't budge, but Kayla crumpled to the side like a Victorian woman on a fainting couch. "What the frig!" I said to Johann. "Back off."

His eyes were black disks. "This is too much. You bring this exquisite flower here and expect me not to pluck her?"

"Nobody's plucking anybody, Johann!" I smacked his shoulder, which was hard as marble. "Ouch!" I shook the pain out of my fingers. "What's going on with you?"

Kayla pushed herself up, her large eyes looming through the blonde locks that had fallen across her face.

"I cannot help myself," he announced, his hands pressed over his long-dead heart.

"Oh, for the love of Jenny Greenteeth," Tarren muttered. She stomped over, flicked her fingers at Kayla, and commanded, "Sleep!" Kayla immediately slumped with her eyes closed. Then Tarren turned to me. "Look, Josie, you're obviously a really nice person and you have some kind of helping complex, but this isn't *Scooby-Doo* and we aren't crighting fime." She looked side to side, trying to figure out what she'd just said. "I mean, fighting crime. You don't know this girl and if she's a runaway, she's not the kind of person we want to get mixed up with. People like that . . ."

"People like what?" I huffed. "You don't even know her!"

"I've known her for eternity," Johann declared. "I've only been waiting to meet her all of my life."

"Johann, put a sock in it!" I told him.

"Tarren's right," Avis said. "She's obviously not in the most stable situation and . . ."

"I can't believe this is coming out of your mouths! You of all people," I said.

Tarren reared back. "Why?"

"You know what it feels like to be different. To be in a situation that you can't control. To not get along with your family. To be in a place where there are all these rules that you have to follow that don't make sense. Kayla and the other girls at HAG are no different than that. Except they don't have any power and they need help!"

"Join the freakin' club," Tarren snapped.

"There's a Vrachnas there," Helios said. He dropped yet another chicken bone into the basket. Johann, Avis, and Tarren stared at him. "You know, sleep demon, wraith, Mora. Some creepy lady demon sucking the souls out of the girls when they sleep. You guys have those?"

"Succubus," Tarren said quietly.

"You go suck a bus," I said to Tarren. "Whatever that means. This is serious business."

"No, you moron, it's called a succubus by the faeries. And an incubus if it's a guy," Tarren said. "But usually they want to, you know, get it on. Maybe this one goes both ways?"

"Witch-riding," said Avis. "That's what folks down south call it."

"Meine schoene damen!" Johann roared. "I will defeat any who try to harm her!" The love zombies jumped at the sound of his voice and began muttering to themselves, but we ignored his histrionics.

"You think that's what happening at HAG?" Tarren asked Helios.

"That's what she described," he said.

For just a moment, I thought Tarren was going to soften. Something about her face relaxing into a half-second of pity. She caught me staring at her and said, "Big freakin' whoop-de-doo. It ain't my problem."

"It should be!" I almost shouted. "Isn't that what everyone's most afraid of? Isn't that why there are all these stupid rules put on you? Because a para could go rogue and hurt humans?" I felt the old Josie rearing up. The one who liked to fight the good fight. And get other people excited about it, too. Only this time I didn't try to squash it. I let Old Josie and New Josie meld. "Only paras like you guys, the good ones, have to suffer under all of this BS because a few bad ones, like that crazy woman who runs HAG, ruins it for everyone. You could rectify that." I stood up and slammed my hands on the table. "You could be the ones who show that paras and humans can help each other and live in peace. This is your chance to prove you aren't monsters!"

"Who you calling a monster?" Avis wanted to know.

Tarren rolled her eyes at me. "Settle down, already. Don't get your pom-poms in a twist."

"Ugh." I fell back into the seat and glared up at Tarren. "Okay, how about this—you'd get to kick some-body's butt and you wouldn't even get in trouble."

Tarren whipped around and glared at me as if she wanted to turn me into an ashtray. "First off, werepire-girl, there's scarier stuff in the world than some random ghoul nibbling on a few runaways and secondly, you have no idea what we're up against with the Council. They could be in on it for all you know."

"No way," I said, but the idea sent a chill through me. I didn't know enough about this Council and from the way everyone talked about them, they scared me.

"Shhh," Avis hissed at her. He craned his neck to look around the room. Then he tugged her into the seat next to him. "Tare, baby, you have to be careful. They could have spies in here."

"Oh come on!" I said, but I looked over my shoulder. "Spies?"

"Josie," Helios said, "somehow your parents have protected you from the Council. Probably because you have no power, so they figured why bother, but the rest of us have to be careful. We're already on probation. The stakes are high."

"But, you guys!" I leaned in and looked around my circle of friends. "If we exposed a nefarious demon, like Maron or Atonia or whoever is hurting those girls, then wouldn't the Council be grateful? Maybe they'd even release you early from anger management." They looked at each other, weighing my words and I was pretty sure I'd convinced them. The old Josie charm still worked, apparently. Not bad for a werepire. "So?" I asked. "Are you in?"

Tarren snorted. "Not a chance!"

"Avis?" I asked.

He shook his head. "Josie, I love ya, but no can do. I don't want to be the only black guy in Saskatchewan."

"Helios?"

He shrugged and pointed to the snoozing Kayla. "I already did my part."

I looked at Johann. "Obviously you're going to help me."

He shrank in the booth and hunched his shoulders, "Well," he said in his mealy-mouthed whiny way. "I've got a lot going on right now and it's very hot outside and . . ."

"What is this? Diary of a Wimpy Vampire?"

He shrugged.

I tossed up my hands. "Oh forget it! I'll just do it myself."

"Sounds like a plan," Tarren said, which made Avis snicker.

"Can one of you at least take Kayla for the night?" I asked, slumping in my seat defeated. "She can't go back to HAG."

"You got her out, you take her," Tarren said.

"I would, but my parents will call the 'appropriate authorities' "—I did finger quotes—"and the whole thing will be botched."

"Obviously she can't come with me or Avis," Helios said.

Johann watched her like a lion licking its chops over a lamb. He opened his mouth to speak but I shut him down before the words were out. "No way," I said.

"Nice try, bat-boy," said Avis.

That left Tarren. I stared at her. She crossed her arms and stared back at me. I thought of all the people who were scattered around her porch and in her yard. "Don't do it, Josie," she warned.

"Don't make me, Tarren," I said.

"I'm not going to offer," she said.

"Then you put me in the position of asking." She closed her eyes and looked away as if I was going to slap her. "Tarren," I said, "can Kayla please stay with you?"

"Yes, of course," she answered quietly. Then she whipped her head around and narrowed her eyes. "One night. That's it. I won't babysit any longer."

"Thank you for the faerie hospitality," I said.

Tarren flipped me off then flicked her fingers at Kayla. "Wake!"

Kayla blinked, rubbed her hands across her face and sat up straight. "Sorry," she said, embarrassed. "I must have dozed off."

The sleep had done her a lot of good. She looked more like her radiant self, which of course sent Johann into a frenzy. He reached over me to paw at her. "You have awoken!"

Kayla smiled uncertainly at Johann then cut her eyes toward me. I shrugged and tried to knock his hand away, but he had me pinned against the back of the booth as he groped for Kayla.

He leaned across me. "We cannot be friends," he said to her in a low voice.

"Um," she said, bewildered. "Okay."

"Trust me," he nearly growled. "You must stay away from me for your own good."

"No problem," she said and stood.

"Are you frightened of me?" he asked.

She narrowed her eyes and shook her head. "No, but you're kind of freaking me out."

"Jeez, Johann!" I pushed against him. "Would you get off me and stop acting like such a *putz*?"

He was up and around the booth before Kayla took a step. "Where are you going, my sweet?"

She frowned and stepped around him then pointed toward the back of Buffy's. "To the bathroom."

"Ah!" He swept aside and bowed deeply. "You always surprise me!" he said with a chuckle.

Kayla looked over her shoulder at him and grimaced then hurried to the ladies' room, but she stopped short by the love zombies. "Bethany?" she said. "Is that you?" One of the girls, a brunette, stared up at her with hollow, searching eyes.

She looked vaguely familiar to me. I tried to place her. Did she go to my high school or was she on another cheerleading team? Then I realized that I'd seen her staring at me a hundred times. "Isn't that girl on those Zombie Apparel billboards?" I asked, but no one answered.

Kayla grabbed the girl's shoulders. "It's me, Kayla. Don't you recognize me?"

The girl shook her head and turned back to the others.

"Oh my god," Kayla wailed. "What did they do to you?"

chapter 14

Kayla clutched my arm and pointed. "That's Bethany. From the shelter. The first one who disappeared. Remember I told you about her?"

I stood, dumbfounded. I had no idea what to think.

Kayla squatted beside the girl's chair and spoke to her quietly. "Bethany, you know who I am. We shared a room. I lent you my clothes. Then you disappeared. Where did you go? What happened? Do you know where Rhonda went? I've been so worried." She reached out and put her arms around the zombie girl's shoulders to hug her, but the girl grunted and swatted Kayla away with more force than I would have thought given her skinny arms. Kayla stumbled backward and the zombie girl blinked her big haunted eyes then turned away.

"They did this to you!" Kayla said loudly. "Sucked the life out of you and turned you into some kind of monster!" Then she crumpled to the ground and wailed,

"Did they do the same thing to Rhonda and Sadie?" An eerie hush fell over Buffy's as everyone focused on the freak out. Tarren and I exchanged glances, but before we could come to some decision about what the heck to do, Johann swooped down. He scooped Kayla up in his arms and headed for the door, which shocked Kayla into a gaped-mouth, blinking silence. The whole thing was weird but it verged on romantic until Johann, the dorkiest dancing vampire ever, tripped. A collective gasp hovered in the air as he stumbled forward, tottering to the left then right, knocking chairs and tables to the ground while Kayla flailed in his grip.

"Ouch! Oh! *Acht!*" Johann hopped on one foot, clutching his left shin with his left hand and half-dragging Kayla across the floor with his right. She managed to get one foot down and hopped along with him as if they were in the worst three legged race ever. Avis, Helios, Tarren, and I ran, tripping over the chairs and tables left in Johann's wake of destruction, trying to reach them before someone ended up in the emergency room. But a spilled soda did them in. Like a clown on a banana peel, Johann's foot hit the puddle then he was airborne, one leg up like a Rockette in mid-kick, the other searching uselessly for the ground. Kayla flew, her mouth a perfect O. They landed, Johann on his back, Kayla splattered on top of him like a broken egg. Without a word, Tarren and I untangled Kayla's limbs from Johann's and slung her arms over our shoulders. Avis and Helios did the same with Johann. We pushed through the doors, carrying our friends outside, just as everyone in Buffy's erupted into laughter.

Kayla curled up on a love seat on Tarren's porch with Johann hovering behind her protectively. Despite his fall, only his ego seemed bruised. "Bethany was at HAG when I first got there," Kayla said. "She went missing a few days later, but I just figured she wanted out of there."

"Who wouldn't?" I said as I settled into a big wicker rocker across from her.

She clicked through pictures on her phone until she landed on one of a cute, perky brunette. "That's her."

I stared at it and frowned. The girl in Buffy's looked like a shadow of the girl on the screen. "Doesn't look like her," I told Kayla. "The girl at Buffy's looks like that model on those billboards."

"It's her for sure," Kayla said. "See that birthmark?" She zoomed in on the girl's face to a half-moon shaped brown splotch on her right cheek.

"I didn't see a birthmark on the girl in Buffy's." Once again I wondered if maybe Kayla was a little bit crazy after all.

"I did," she said. Then she clicked through more pictures. "Here's Rhonda." She showed me a gorgeous girl with dark skin and cornrows ending in bright beads. "And here's Sadie."

"God, she's a baby," I said as I worried over the picture of the petite girl with straight dark hair, olive skin, and two eyebrow rings.

"She's fifteen," Kayla said.

Tarren came out of the house carrying a tray with a pitcher and six glasses. She set them on the coffee table and poured everyone a big drink of butterfly milk. I accepted my cup and graciously took a huge swig. Immediately my arms and legs relaxed and nothing seemed quite as bad as it did two minutes ago.

"We could use the pictures to make missing-person flyers," I said. "I could also post the pix on Facebook and my blog, too."

"You have a blog?" Tarren asked, drawing out the last word so it sounded like she was retching.

A flush crawled up my neck as I realized that I had never rewritten what I posted about the paras after I first met them. "Hardly anybody reads it," I mumbled.

"That's not true!" Kayla said. "Josie's blog is awesome. Everyone at HAG reads it religiously." Then her face clouded over as if she might be putting something together.

Tarren scoffed. "So you're a goddess now, Josephine? Helios's parents will be thrilled."

Avis cackled from his perch on the porch railing. The overhead light flickered. We all gawked at Helios who glowered at Tarren and Avis from the steps.

"I'm just playing," Tarren said to Helios. "You really should get a sense of humor one of these days."

"Some things aren't funny." Helios stood and began to walk toward the front gate.

"You're leaving?" I called after him.

"Would you like a ride home?" he said over his shoulder.

I wasn't sure if that was Greek god hospitality or if he really wanted to give me a ride, but I wasn't waiting to find out. I grabbed my stuff then I took Kayla's hand. "Will you be okay?"

She looked at me, then turned to look at Johann. She hesitated but then she smiled. "I think I'll be just fine."

Johann announced, "I will not leave her side."

"Coming on a little strong there, Yo," I told him. "You might want to back it up."

"You should definitely take that ride," Kayla said, and I ran after Helios.

Helios and I rode in comfortable silence to my house, which was nice. I never had that with Kevin. Either he blared the music or we had a billion other people in the car with us or he would yammer about whatever was most interesting to him, which was usually himself. Sometimes I wondered why I was so into that guy. He probably liked me because I liked him, but why I liked him was still a mystery to me. I always thought we were having fun, but maybe we were just distracting ourselves from the fact that we didn't have much in common beyond hanging out in the same circle of idiots at school.

As we neared my house, images of almost kissing Helios at the stoplight floated through my mind and I wondered whether that was a just passing moment, or if it could happen again . . . and if I wanted it to.

"Crazy night," he said as he pulled into my driveway.

"Yeah, I guess so." We sat quietly for a minute then I said, "Are you really not going to help me figure out what's happening to those girls?"

He turned toward me and laid his hand on top of mine, which made my heart rev. "We're not superheroes, Josie. We're just a bunch of wussies with weird powers we're not allowed to use. It might seem cool, but it's not."

"It could be," I said.

He let go of my hand and shook his head. "You don't get it."

"Then explain it to me," I said.

"I don't know if I can." Helios killed the engine and settled into his seat. The motion sensor light on our garage timed out and we were left sitting in the moonlight filtering through the oak tree in my front yard. He peered out the windshield toward my house. "Do you have brothers and sisters?"

"Nope, just me," I said.

"Must be very calm at your house."

"Like a funeral parlor."

"Sounds nice."

"Seriously?" I looked over at our little yellow house with its neatly trimmed yard and begonia-filled window boxes. "I've always thought it was the most boring place on the planet."

"Do you know how many brothers and sisters I have?" he asked. I shook my head. "Literally hundreds."

My mouth dropped open.

"That's what happens when your father is a) immortal and b) an a-hole. And he expects me to be just like him. Carry on the endless family tradition of Helioses. Go back to Greece, find a nice pure-bred goddess . . ."

"Aha," I said. "That's why Tarren and Avis irritated you so much with their stupid joke."

"Tarren of all people should understand the pressure a family can put on one. Anyway I don't want to marry a goddess and have kids then go fool around fathering more children with dozens of different women. He's such a freakin' hypocrite." The night sky flickered with heat lightning. "Shove it!" Helios yelled. "He's the one who outed Aphrodite and Ares for sleeping together while he was messing around with anything he could screw, both mortal and immortal."

"Sheesh, I wish someone like him had been around when my ex was screwing my best friend. If I had just asked Chloe the right questions . . ." I trailed off as I relived Kevin coming out of the car, pulling up his pants. Madison in the backseat staring at me. Me with a bat in my hands. It all seemed so stupid.

"I would have told you," Helios said.

"I might have avoided the whole anger management thing then."

"But you wouldn't have met me," Helios said with a sly grin.

"That's true." I cracked a smile. "Maybe it was worth it."

Helios reached out and touched my hand again. "I'm not like them, you know. I don't play around like they do."

"Like Kevin?"

"Your ex. My father and my half brothers and cousins. All them going way back to the first. They're all the same guy. But I'm not one of them."

I leaned on the console between us and stared at his dreamy profile. "I can see that." Before I knew what I was doing, I reached out and touched the side of his perfect face. "You're amazing."

"Appearances can be deceiving," he said with a sigh, but I cut him off.

"It's not just how you look, it's who you are," I said. "With your friends, you're kind and thoughtful. And you can be passionate. You stick up for what you believe."

He looked at me. "Are you trying to sweet-talk me into helping you again?"

I laughed. "Maybe a little bit, but only because I believe that everything I'm saying is true."

Helios laid his hand on my shoulder. It was warm like the sun. "You're pretty amazing yourself, Josie Griffin."

I shook my head. "Merely mortal."

"You don't know how hot that is."

I leaned one way. He leaned the other. We both closed our eyes and then we kissed. As soon as my tongue found his, the world illuminated. Literally. The overhead light in the car popped on, the dashboard lit up, and the garage light blazed through the windshield.

"Sorry," Helios said, pulling away. The lights dimmed but I could see that he was embarrassed by the display.

I laughed. "I've never had that effect on a guy before."

He shifted in the seat. "It's late. I should get going."

I pecked him on the cheek one last time. "Thanks again for your help today. And if you change your mind . . ." I opened the door and stepped halfway out, then I turned back to him. "You know where to find me."

I KISSED A GREEK GOD!

That was what I wrote for my blog post when I got inside. I reread the words then fell back into the pillows on my bed. In the past, I would have been on the phone with Madison or Chloe parsing every detail of the kiss, what we said, how it felt, what my next move should be. We did that endlessly whenever one of us started dating a new guy. When I hooked up with Kevin, I confided all of my feelings to them and told them every detail of our relationship. But at some point, Madison must have been doing the same thing. And Chloe would have been listening to Madison and me gush over the same guy. I grabbed a pillow and squeezed it against my aching chest. I thought Madison was listening to me, advising me, rooting for me, but really she was gathering info to betray me. And Chloe chose the cheaters over me. If only I lived in a Greek tragedy, I could have gotten justice!

I sat up and erased the words on my screen. I couldn't post about kissing Helios. And not just because I'd sound freaky if I claimed I made out with an actual god. But more because I didn't feel like blabbing about it to anyone else. It felt personal and maybe kind of special. In fact, I decided then and there that I would take down my blog post about the paras because it wasn't fair for me to be blathering on and on about their lives. But first, I'd promised that I would help Kayla. I checked my email and found pix she'd sent of all the missing girls so I got busy designing flyers with their names and my cell phone number. I printed twenty then I got to work blasting the web with info about the girls. I might not have superpowers, but I knew how to network online.

On my blog, I posted the pix of the girls and asked for help from anyone who had info. Then, even though I'd unfriended almost everyone I know, I went ahead and posted on Facebook because it couldn't hurt to ask people to spread the word. Finally I got up my nerve to send an email to my idol, Graham Goren at *Nuevo Indy*. If anyone would go after a story about girls going missing from the same shelter, he would. The last thing I did was look at the Center for Missing and Exploited Children website.

Searching the Indiana database of missing people for endangered runaways almost broke my heart. There were dozens of kids who had vanished from all over the state. At first I scrolled through the lists quickly, but then I slowed down and looked hard at each face. What happened, I wondered, to make their lives so bad? As I was doing this I came across a picture of a girl named Eleanor. She had a round face, thick brownish-blonde hair pulled in a ponytail, and bright blue eyes. She was smiling with her mouth half open as if she had been laughing. There was something about her that was familiar, but there was no way I could know her. She was from Elkhart, which is in northern Indiana. I'd only been there for regional cheerleading competitions. I read her info. She was seventeen, my age. Five feet five inches tall. My height. She weighed almost the same as me, too. We had the same hair color. Her eyes were blue and mine were green and she had a butterfly tattoo on her wrist, but other than that, we were so much alike. At that moment, I felt some strange kinship with this girl. What my grandmother might have called *There but for the grace of God go I.* I never understood what she meant until that moment. But I realized then that if Kevin had been an even bigger jerk and my parents less understanding, I could have easily been an Eleanor—the kind of girl who got in trouble over a guy and had nowhere to turn so she took off.

It really sucked that the paras wouldn't help me, but I knew if I put my mind to it, I could figure out what was happening to all those girls. I got back online and posted more pix until I fell asleep, slumped over my laptop.

chapter 15

the first thing I did the next morning was check my blog for any comments with news about the girls. Nothing. Then I checked Facebook. Nothing. I knew I needed to go back through my blog and take out my posts about the paras, but first I checked my email and about fell over when I saw a message from Graham Goren, *the* Graham Goren! My hero at *Nuevo Indy* was actually emailing me back

> Hi Josie,
>
> Thanks for your email. I'm interested in learning more about this story. Can I give you a call?
>
> Best,
>
> Graham

Hells yes! I zinged a message back to him with my

cell number and told him to call anytime. Then I got a text. I ran for the phone, thinking it might be Graham, but it was from Kayla. *Come hang out!* she said and I actually squealed with excitement like a dorky eight-year-old who got her first slumber party Evite. Guess it'd been a while since anyone texted me to hang out. *B there soon!* I texted back.

I wondered if Helios would be there. I started punching in a text to him, *R U going to . . .* then I stopped. Did it matter if he would be there? I erased half of the text then I stopped again. Maybe it shouldn't matter if he would be there, but it did. I punched the words in again. I stopped. At least I could play it cool. I erased and started over. *Heading to Tarren's. You coming?* I hesitated before I hit SEND. Maybe they all went there every day and now I sounded like an idiot. Or maybe he was still irritated with Tarren and Avis and he never wanted to go there again. Or maybe the fact that I was going to be there would make him want to come. Or maybe I could write the most boring book in the universe that catalogued the minutia of my crush on a supernatural guy and make a billion dollars!

I moaned and banged the phone against my forehead. This was when a girl needed a best friend or at least a blog to help her figure out what to do. But I didn't have time to post all this nonsense so finally I punched in *Going to Tarren's. What's up with you?* I hit SEND before I second guessed myself and I didn't wait for a reply. Luckily my dad had picked up my car from the mechanic and so I grabbed a fistful of flyers and headed out in Gladys for the day.

"Look what I have," I announced, waving the papers, as I walked up Tarren's porch steps. Kayla and Tarren were sprawled, still in their pajamas, across two couches with newspaper sections scattered on the floor between them while Avis was perched right where I left him last night on the porch rail, only this time he was playing Angry Birds on his phone. I wondered if he ever left. Helios unfortunately was nowhere to be seen.

Tarren sat up and took a flyer from me. "This is good," she said. "We should plaster the hood with them."

I plopped down beside her. "So now you'll help?"

"Of course I will," she said. She looked over at Kayla who was studying the flyers. "Anything for my girl, KK."

Kayla looked up and thumped her heart with a fist then pointed at Tarren. "Blood," she said, and they both giggled.

"Did I miss something?" I asked.

Avis rolled his eyes. "Don't even try," he told me. "It's like they've got their own secret society all a sudden." He hopped down from the rail awkwardly and strutted across the porch. "If you ask me, it was staying up all night drinking butterfly milk. That stuff will mess you up if you're not careful."

"Shut up," Tarren said playfully. "KK and I have a lot in common."

"We formed the American Association for Dyslexics with Idiots for Parents," said Kayla.

"AADIP for short," Tarren said and they both cracked up again.

Avis and I looked at each other. I could tell he felt as left out as I did, but I was used to this kind of thing. Madison and Chloe ganged up and excluded me all the time then, just when I'd get pissed, they'd back off and beg me not to be mad. It should have come as no surprise that they teamed up in the end.

"Are you both really dyslexic?" I asked, as if it mattered. But I didn't hear their answer because my phone beeped. I slipped it out of my pocket and saw a text from Helios. *Sorry. Family stuff came up. What M I missing?*

As I started to type a reply, the front gate squeaked open and we heard, "I have returned!" We all looked up and our mouths dropped open as Johann swaggered up the walkway. His waist-high jeans were stonewashed, his T-shirt said *RELAX* in big neon pink letters, and for some reason he'd pushed up the sleeves and turned up the collar of his boxy black blazer. Not only that, but he seemed to have inexplicably grown a mullet overnight and was wearing big, ugly aviator sunglasses.

I snapped a picture and texted it to Helios with the caption, *This is what you're missing.*

"What's up with that?" Tarren snorted when Johann got to the porch.

"With what?" Johann asked.

My phone beeped again. Helios's text said, *Notice anything unusual about Santa Carla yet?*

I howled.

"What's wrong with you?" Tarren asked.

"Nothing, nothing," I said, trying to control my laughter as I texted Helios back, *OMG my aunt JoJo LOVES The Lost Boys! She made me watch it a zillion times. Johann is so Corey Haim!*

Johann looked down at his own clothes as if he was second guessing himself, but Kayla saved him. "You look awesome!" Kayla said. "I totally love retro. Especially the 80s."

My mouth fell open. If I didn't know better, I would have thought she was flirting with him.

Then Kayla pulled Tarren off the couch. "Come on," she said. "Let's get dressed."

As she passed, Johann inhaled deeply. His eyes were closed and his tongue darted from between his lips. It was the same look I remembered on his mother's face when she wanted me for an appetizer.

Once the girls were inside, I smacked him on the back of the head, sending his sunglasses flying. "What the H are you doing?"

He caught his sunglasses before they hit the ground. "You have no idea how much I crave her," he said.

"Yo, you can't hang with us if you keep acting a fool around that girl," Avis said.

Johann whipped around to face Avis. His upturned collar and shoulder pads made him appear larger. He stepped closer to Avis. "You want her also," he accused. "I can see it in your eyes. The way you look at her. A wolf lurking in the shadows."

Avis shook his head. "Dang, Johann. I'm not interested in that girl. I have more than I can handle with Tarren."

"You cannot keep me from her," Johann declared. "I am drawn to her."

Avis crossed his arms. "I'll tell Charles."

Johann shrank a little and pleaded, "No, no, don't do that."

"Just be cool, Johann," I said. "Kayla's really laid back. If you keep coming on this strong, you're going to scare her away."

Kayla came out the front door in Tarren's clothes—short shorts and a tiny tee with butterflies across the front. Johann rushed to her side. "Have I frightened you?"

Kayla laughed. "Don't be silly. You're, like, the cutest little thing I've ever seen." He dropped to his knees and grabbed her hand then pressed it to his lips. She yelped and yanked her hand away. "Jesus you're cold! You must have terrible circulation."

"Alas," Johann said, hanging his head. "That is true."

"I don't mind," Kayla said and reached for him again. "I can warm you up."

They stared into each other's eyes longer than necessary. Part of me wanted to tell them to get a room and another part wanted to slap Johann upside the head again and knock some sense into Kayla. Maybe he couldn't help his preternatural attraction to Kayla, but what was her deal? She couldn't possibly find him so hot, could she? He was such a dork.

Johann reached for Kayla. "Would you like to go dancing with me?"

Especially when he said things like that.

Kayla blushed and stammered because what girl in her right mind would say yes to that?

"Yes," she said, and I realized then that maybe Kayla wasn't in her right mind after all. Or maybe Johann had found someone on whom his mind tricks worked.

Luckily I wasn't the only one who found them annoying. Tarren got tired of their puppy-dog eyes. "Are we going to do this or not?" she said, waving a flyer between them, breaking their trance.

"Of course," Kayla said, looking away from Johann. "Anything to help my girls."

"And anything to help you," added Johann.

We walked the streets of Tarren's neighborhood, hanging flyers on lampposts every block. Whenever we saw someone, we showed them the pictures and asked if they'd seen the missing girls. No one had. When we were almost out of flyers, we were near an elementary school yard with a basketball court.

"Hey!" Kayla said, jogging across the grassy field to an abandoned ball sitting sadly on the sidelines. "Who's up for some hoops?"

Tarren, Avis, and Johann stopped at edge of the court. We all looked at each other nervously.

"They're really bad at basketball," I told Kayla. "I already tried to play with them."

"Who cares!" Kayla said, dribbling toward the basket. "It's just for fun." She stopped at the top of the key and shot. The ball swooshed through the net. She grinned at us. "Starting forward, Evansville South High School girls b-ball team." As she retrieved the ball from the grass, three guys appeared around the corner of the school.

"Uh-oh," I said and pointed.

Drey, the neighborhood menace, strutted to the court. "Yo," he said. "Who wants to play ball?"

"Actually . . ." Avis shifted uncomfortably. "We were just leaving."

"Don't start, Drey," Tarren warned.

"You don't have worry about me," Drey said. "I'm just being friendly." Then his eyes landed on Kayla who held the ball against her hip. "Hello there, Miss Thing."

Johann moved at warp speed, sending his mullet aflutter. He wedged himself between Drey and Kayla. "She is with us," he growled.

"So, why don't you have some manners and introduce her?" Drey asked.

"Um, um," Johann stammered and stepped back. He took off his sunglasses and began a very formal introduction. "Kayla, this is Tarren's neighbor Drey. Drey, this is Kayla." Drey reached for Kayla's hand but when their fingers touched, Johann snarled.

Drey shot Tarren a look. "Your friend got a problem? Only reason he's still standing up is 'cause he's with you."

Tarren rolled her eyes. "Let's not start something," she said and fluttered between them, pushing Johann farther away. "Hey, Drey, you seen these girls?" She handed him a flyer.

Drey studied it for a few seconds then shook his head. "Nah. Wouldn't mind to meet this one." He pointed to Rhonda. "She's fine." Then he turned back to Kayla and winked. "Not as fine as you though."

Tarren shot Drey a warning glance, but Kayla laughed. Johann clenched his fists at his side.

"You sure?" Tarren asked. "They're missing."

"Well, they ain't on the street selling something, I can tell you that. If they was, I'd know for sure. My cousin Big Ron runs this hood and I know every girl working out here." He turned back to Kayla. "You looking for a job, honey?"

Johann sprang, like a Doberman. Drey saw him coming. He hopped to the side and threw an elbow, sending Johann crashing to the concrete. He landed on the side of his foot then rolled to his back, clutching his ankle. "Ow! Oh! Ow!" he cried.

"For the love of Jenny Greenteeth," Tarren huffed. "Again, Johann? This is getting ridiculous. And you!" she yelled at Drey. "Haven't I warned you not to mess with my friends?"

While Avis and I were trying to decide whether to help Johann or keep Tarren from zapping Drey, Kayla draped herself over the moaning vampire. "Was that the same ankle you hurt the other night? You poor baby," she cooed to him. "Do you think you can stand up?"

"No," Johann winced, but it looked to me that he was faking. "I must have sprained something."

"I'm gonna sprain your damn face for trying to jump me like that, fool!" Drey yelled. His buddies loomed up like shadows.

Avis reached out and held Tarren back. "Keep cool, baby," he warned, but then Drey grabbed Kayla by the arm and pushed her away from Johann. Tarren was ready to pounce, though Kayla didn't need her help. She punched Drey hard on the shoulder and yelled, "Get your hands off me!" Then she started cursing up a blue streak.

"Hey!" Tarren yelled. She wriggled between the three guys and our friends. "Everyone just dettle sown!"

Drey towered over tiny Tarren, yelling his own string of obscenities back at Kayla who hadn't stopped hurling insults. Then Avis stepped in, his elbows back, chest puffed forward, and I could have sworn a line of red dreadlocks rose off his scalp like a rooster's comb.

I watched the whole thing, frozen, unsure what to do to help until the guy to Drey's left slipped something out of his back pocket. The sun glinted off the object. "A knife!" I screamed. "He's got a knife behind his back!"

Tarren whipped around. As if in slo-mo, her lips worked, searching for the right words. Trying to find a way to force them into the air. She threw her arms toward the three guys and shouted, "Freak Sneeze!"

Drey's head snapped back. The others followed suit. They sucked in air, *"Ah! Ah! Ah!"* as if gathering force. *"Ah! Ah! Ah!"* Instinctively I closed my eyes, threw my arm in front of my face, and turned away as all three guys exploded. *"CHEW-EW-EW-EW-EW!"* The sound of the enormous sneezes ricocheted across the basketball court, bounced off the school walls, and echoed into the trees and houses surrounding us. Their heads snapped back again. Drey convulsed in a series of quick relentless sneezes, *"Achooachooachooachoo!"* The guy with the shiny thing stumbled around sucking in air again, *"Ah! Ah! Ah!"* as the other guy tried to pick himself up off the ground where his epic sneeze had left him, but as soon as he got to his knees, he was thrown forward by another huge explosion of snot and spit.

That gave Kayla just enough time to grab Johann. She pulled him to his feet. He let out a cry of pain as he put weight on his ankle so Kayla crouched down in front of him and yelled, "Hop on!" Johann looked confused but then he took hold of her shoulders, jumped, and wrapped his legs around her waist. "Nothing can come between us!" he yelled. Kayla took off running across the grassy field with Johann bouncing on her back.

Another gigantic sneeze erupted from the three guys. Then another.

"Tarren!" I screamed. "They're going to pop a head vein. Do something!"

"Snow knees! Snow knees!" she shouted.

The three guys all started shaking as their kneecaps

turned white and frosty and they continued sneezing up a storm.

"I mean, no sneeze!" Tarren added. "And no snow knees!" she shouted, flinging her arms their way.

All three of them collapsed to the ground, panting and moaning. Avis swooped down and grabbed the shiny object in the grass. He held it up and looked at me with bulging eyes.

"Oops!" I said when I saw the cell phone. "Guess I was wrong."

"Go, go, go!" he yelled, pushing Tarren and me away. "Get the heck out of here."

He threw the phone and we ran for the school. We ducked around the corner then Tarren yelled, "Wait! Wait." She peeked around the side of the building and flung her arms toward the guys, shouting "Forget! Forget!" at the top of her lungs. We pressed our backs against the wall then all three of us poked our heads out to see Drey and his boys wobbling to their feet.

"What the!" Drey yelled. "What happened?" He clutched his forehead and rubbed his bright red knees and moaned.

"Dang, man, how did we get here?" The guy with the phone shook his head as if to clear it. "Did we smoke something?"

"Smoke!" the other one said, rubbing the sides of his nose. "We must have snorted some crazy thing."

"And why are my knees killing me?" the other guy said.

"I'm gonna find whoever sold us whatever it was we took and kick his ass!" Drey said.

They staggered off in the opposite direction. Avis, Tarren, and I looked at each other and busted up.

"Oh my god!" I said. "What kind of spell was that?"

Tarren could barely catch her breath, she was giggling so much. She clutched her sides and said, "That's not what I meant! I was trying to make him freeze. I thought he was sneaking out a knife. But my brain got all confused. Sneak? Freeze? Which was the right word? I couldn't spit it out right. I got all jumbled and it came out freak sneeze and then instead of *no sneeze*, I yelled *snow knees*!"

Avis and I lost it again.

"I thought it was some kind of ancient faerie curse you were throwing at them," I told her.

"The curse of the freak sneeze and snowy knees!" Tarren boomed in a deep, ominous voice then cracked up again. "Handed down for generations."

"Dang, I thought their eyes were going to pop out of their heads," Avis said. "I thought their noses were gonna fly off their faces and circle the moon. Those were some freaky sneezes all right." Then he slung his arm around Tarren's slim shoulders. "You're something else, Tarren baby." He kissed the top of her head. "But at least you saved us from that phone." He looked at me. "What did you think he was going to do, Josie? Post a vid on YouTube of Johann getting his booty kicked? Call Big Ron to send some hookers over to beat us senseless with their tube tops?"

"Sorry." I winced. "I thought it was a knife. I got a little carried away."

"So did Johann," Tarren said, and we all cracked up again. "Where do you think they're off to?"

"Oh my god, I have to tell Helios this." I pulled out my phone and started texting him about the piggyback ride and mixed-up hexes.

"Where is he anyway?" Tarren asked.

I shrugged. "Some family thing came up." I caught a weird, worried look between Tarren and Avis. "What?" I asked, mid-text.

"Nothing," Avis said. "His family can be . . ." he trailed off.

"Difficult," Tarren finished.

"You think he's okay?" I asked, my thumb hovering over the SEND button.

"Sure," Avis said. "Our boy can take care of himself." He paused and then added, "And if he can't, we'll just send Kayla in for him." He snickered again. "That girl picked up Johann and slung him on her back like she was a mama gorilla running from a lion! And he's all bouncing around yelling, 'Nothing can separate us!' like he was the one doing the rescuing."

Tarren nodded her head and beamed. "Yeah, I told you my girl KK is all right."

"Your girl?" I asked. "You didn't even want to help her yesterday."

Tarren shrugged. "That was before I knew her."

"And now?" I asked.

She looked out over the grassy field where Kayla trotted off with Johann on her back. "Well, now, I guess, I sort of . . ."

I filled in the blank. "Want to help?"

She looked at me. "Not you, Josie," she said. "I want to help *her*."

chapter 16

On the way back to Tarren's to find Johann and Kayla, we turned a corner and were across the street from HAG. Tarren grabbed Avis and me by the elbows and yanked us behind a big sycamore tree. "We need more information about that place," she said.

"I tried Googling it . . ." I peeked around the tree at the nondescript cement block building.

"For spriggan's sake," Tarren said. "How many times do I have to tell you that the Internet is not a good source of information."

"Are you out of your mind?!" I said. "Do you know how many websites are dedicated to stuff like this? My old boyfriend always went to this demon hunter site and—"

Avis cut me off. "The stuff you find online is not authentic, Josie. You can't hunt a ghost with a phone app. You can't build a demon-o-meter with a DustBuster and a satellite dish. Real paras keep as low a profile as possible. You're not going to find pix of the latest shape-shifter reunion at the Marriot posted on Facebook. We just don't do it."

"Well," I said at a loss. "Then how do you propose we get more info then, the library?"

Tarren stared at me, waiting.

"I was joking about the library," I muttered, but she kept on staring. "What?"

"You have to go in there, Josie," she told me.

"Me? Why me? What am I going do?"

Tarren flittered around me like a sweaty bee. "You're the only one who has access. Kayla can't go back yet. She'd be in danger. You know that. And Avis can't go waltzing in there. Helios has already been in. And Johann . . . ?" She stopped and rolled her eyes.

"You do it, then," I said. "Now that you're Miss Helpy McHelpson. BFF with KK."

Tarren sighed. She reached out and laid her small hand on my arm. "Josie," she said sweetly. "Please don't be jealous of my friendship with Kayla. She's your friend, too. We all want to help, but obviously I have no legitimate reason to go inside. You, however, have the perfect excuse! And you'd be so good at it! You can ask questions, snoop a little, interview some of the other girls. Isn't that what investigative reporting is all about?"

I leaned back against the rough bark of the tree and stared at her. "You're reverse Josie-ing me."

"I'm what?" she asked all innocent, but she wasn't an idiot and neither was I.

"Giving me a dose of my own homeo-pathetic remedy," I told her.

She dropped the fairy cheerleader act, crossed her arms, stuck one hip out, and leveled with me. "Okay, look, whatevs. You're right. I'm trying to sweet-talk you, but only because it's such a good idea, so why don't you grow a pair and do it already?"

"What if Ms. Babineaux and Maron know I'm the one who sneaked Kayla out?" I whisper-whined.

Tarren rolled her eyes. "How would they know that? She was with Helios. They don't know Helios. They don't know that you know Helios. So you're safe."

"Okay, but what if there really is some kind of soul-sucking demon in there and I'm its lunch? Why can't you send the paranormal police in there, or call up one of those Council members you're always yammering about?"

"You know we can't do that," Tarren said as if that was the dumbest thing she'd ever heard. "And anyway if there's something in there, it goes for vulnerable girls who've got no one watching out for them. They know you have a family to go home to and a court order to be there. If you go missing, people are going to ask questions. But those girls, Kayla and the others and whoever's next . . ." She trailed off and shook her head. "Who's looking out for them?"

I moaned. She had me. "Hoisted on my own petard," I muttered.

"Who you calling a retard?" Avis asked.

174

"Never mind," I said and I knew then that I was going to do it because she was right. I wouldn't abandon those girls when they needed me. "Fine. But if I'm not back at your place in two hours, you have to call my cell and make sure I'm okay."

"You got it," Avis said.

"Really?" I asked. "Because I'm freaking out over here."

He reached out and patted my shoulder. "We've got your back."

I looked at Tarren. "Me, too," she assured me. Then she thumped her fist against her chest and said, "Blood."

"What are you doing here?" Maron snapped from behind the reception desk when I walked in through the front door.

Good question, what was I doing there? "I, um, can't make my shift later this week," I lied. "So I wanted to do a makeup now. Is that okay?"

She worked her tongue in her mouth like she had got something stuck between her teeth—flesh of girls, perhaps, but then she said, "Yeah, fine, what do I care?" That came as a relief. At least she didn't clock me on the head with a tire iron and drag my body into a dungeon for some demon to consume my essence. At least not yet.

"What would you like me to do?" I asked.

"I've already got someone scrubbing the johns," Maron said. "Why don't you change the sheets?"

. . .

In the utility room, I looked around furtively. Washer. Dryer. Linens. Cleaning supplies. A mop. What was I looking for? It occurred to me that I had no idea. What did we think I'd find? A hidden door in the wall? Secret surveillance tapes? A dead body stuffed in the laundry shoot? Eeeeh. That gave me the shivers. I didn't even want to find that. Plus I was inside a glorified cleaning closet so unless they were Lysoling the girls to death, I wasn't going to find anything concrete to confirm my suspicions. Which meant Tarren was right; I was going to have to think like an investigative reporter.

On my way to the dorm room, I got a text from Helios and I'll admit, my cheeks got warm and my heart sped up when I saw his name on my tiny screen. Ah, distraction! His text said, *I miss all the fun.*

I texted back, *Not all of it. I'm at HAG now.*

A minute later this popped up, *Don't fall asleep on the job, ha-ha!*

Very funny, I texted back. *I'm freaking out!*

In the dorm, all the beds were unmade, except for two, which must have meant that those two beds weren't occupied the night before. I poked my head into the hall. No one was around so I started snooping to confirm my theory. Quietly I riffled through the top drawer of the nightstands beside the made-up beds. In one I found a tattered copy of *Pride and Prejudice and Zombies*, the book Kayla had been reading. Beside the nightstand was a cheap particle board wardrobe. I opened the door and saw jeans, sweatshirts, and blue and green Pumas

176

neatly stowed away. On the top shelf was a duffle bag with Kayla's name on the luggage tag.

In the other nightstand, I found a bunch of trashy magazines but under that I found Sadie's ID card from Bean Blossom High School. I felt queasy looking at her picture. She was so young and sweet. How could anyone ever hurt her? I opened her wardrobe, but it was empty. Only a few wire hangers and a pink sock remained. Everything else, no doubt, had been hauled out to the Dumpster, erasing any evidence that Sadie had ever been here. On impulse, I grabbed the school ID and shoved it in my back pocket. Then I gathered all the linens into a giant laundry bag and dragged it to the washer.

On my way to find sheets to put on the beds, I heard someone cleaning the toilet stalls. I glanced over my shoulder to make sure Maron wasn't watching then I ducked into the bathroom. "Hey there. Who's that?" I called out as I rounded the stall. A pale brunette girl my height peeked around the edge of the stall. She had that same frightened look that Sadie had the last time I saw her, like a little kid in a haunted house. "How's it going?" I asked.

"Fine," she said with no emotion, then she pushed her hair out of her face with the back of her hand and I saw a small tattoo on her wrist.

I gasped and reached for her hand. She instinctively stepped back, but not quickly enough. I pulled her arm straight and looked at the tattoo—a small butterfly. "Is your name Eleanor? Are you from Elkhart?"

The girl stared at me and I thought I saw the slightest glimmer of recognition in her eyes. It reminded me of how my grandfather with Alzheimer's would become lucid for a minute then disappear again into his own lost world.

I stepped closer to her and said quietly, "Do you need help?" but before she could answer, there was a commotion in the hall. I saw Maron pulling Ms. Babineaux past the door toward the reception area.

"A reporter?" Ms. Babineaux asked.

"Some alternative paper," Maron told her.

"Why didn't you get rid of him?" Ms. Babineaux said, but then they were down the hall, so I didn't hear the answer.

As much as I wanted to grill the girl on whether she was the person I saw on the Missing Children website or if she knew Sadie or Rhonda or how she ended up at HAG, I was more interested in knowing what reporter was there. I dropped her arm. "Wait here. I'll be back." Then I headed for the front.

I slipped into the day lounge beside the reception area. The ugly brown plaid couch faced away from the front desk, so I crawled onto it and hid. I could hear whoever was with Ms. Babineaux and Maron, but they couldn't see me. Peeking over the top of the couch, I saw Ms. Babineaux. She looked withered and old again, like she did when I first met her. She was so skinny I could see her pale hip bones poking out from the top of her slacks.

"This is a private facility, buddy," Maron said.

I peeked a little bit higher and saw a man in wire-rimmed glasses and an army jacket. I nearly popped up and shouted, *Graham Goren!* I couldn't believe that my idol from *Nuevo Indy* was standing right there. But I refrained and instead ducked down so I could listen without being detected.

"You receive public funding, don't you?" he asked.

"We're not going to say anything about confidential cases," Ms. Babineaux told him. "That would betray the trust of our girls."

My jaw dropped. Their girls! Barfity barf barf. More like their victims.

"How many facilities do you run?" he asked.

This seemed to catch both of them off guard. Maron stammered then said, "Just this one."

"What about the other Helping American Girls in Fort Wayne and Terre Haute?" he asked.

Maron sputtered, "Oh those? That was a confusing question . . . I didn't know what you meant . . ."

I couldn't help but smile. For me, listening to a good journalist work was like a sports nut watching a slam dunk. Goren kept grilling them. "And about how many girls go missing from each facility a month?"

"Hey look, buddy," Maron said. "The girls who come here are a mess. And this is voluntary. Girls are free to come and go as they please."

"We wish they would all stay until the dedicated staff could get them straightened out but the truth is, many of these girls are on drugs or engage in prostitution or theft," Ms. Babineaux said.

I popped up from the couch. What a crock! Kayla, Rhonda, Sadie, and the other girls didn't do those things. Drey said so. I realized that I was about to blow my cover and I ducked down again.

Maron went on. "I love them all like a mother, but sometimes they decide life on the street is what they want. I can't stop them."

She needed a shovel for all the manure she was slinging! Like a good reporter, Goren seemed skeptical.

"I spoke with several other halfway house facilities in the state and they said they have less than one girl a month take off without informing the staff. But my sources tell me that your average is much higher. Why do you think that is?"

"Your sources?" Ms. Babineaux's voice was stiff. "And just who are these sources?"

There was part of me that wanted to jump over the back of the couch and scream, *ME! I'm the source and I'm on to you, you evil hags.* Then I'd poke my finger into their chests and throw questions at them like a super journalist. Wear them down. Catch one of them in a lie and make her admit the truth. But I remembered what Charles always said about staying calm and assessing the situation before acting. Jumping over a couch would probably not be the best lead-in to questioning. Plus I was such a spaz that I would probably fall over the couch and break my arm, so I sat tight, but oh, my blood was beginning to boil.

"My sources are confidential," Graham Goren said. "But I can say that it's someone who is familiar with your facility from the inside."

"A client or a worker?" Maron asked. Her voice was so ominous. I imagined her cracking her knuckles and rolling her head from left to right, ready to tear the squealer limb from limb. And since that squealer was me, my stomach went all queasy.

"I can't say," Goren told her. Then he changed tacks. "I'd like to talk with some of the girls here," he said, as if it was the most reasonable request in the world.

Ms. Babineaux scoffed. "You most certainly may not. And we have to get back to work so you'll need to go now."

"That's fine," Goren said, all professional and polite. "Thank you for your time."

Whoa. I could never be that calm in a million years. But obviously I was going to have to learn if I want a job like his. I waited until I heard the front door open, then close. I strained my ears to catch what Atonia and Maron were saying, but I heard nothing. Did they leave? Were they following him? Would they unleash an evil succubus to feast on his brain then drag his carcass to the Dumpster? Slowly I rose up from the couch and peered over the edge. I saw them, standing close, whispering, but not before Maron saw me.

"What do you think you're doing here?"

I stood up and said loudly, "I finished the beds!" I grabbed some throw pillows and fluffed them as Atonia and Maron stared at me. "Just straightening up in here now." I tossed the pillows onto the couch. I did an exaggerated glance at the clock. "Wow! Have two hours passed already? I've got to get going. Can't stay long today. I have to leave early. I mentioned that, didn't I?" I babbled on and on as I made a beeline past them straight for the front door. "That was a good productive work day. Doing laundry. All in a good day's work. See you again soon!"

"Hold on just a second," Maron barked right as I reached the door.

I paused with my hand pressed against the glass.

"What's going on here?" Ms. Babineaux asked, as if she was trying to put all the pieces together. Her eyes widened, then they narrowed. If she could shoot fire from her retinas, I would have been a smoking lump of ashes.

I decided I didn't want to be a part of that jigsaw puzzle. "Have to go! Uh, um, dentist appointment. Can't be late!" I said and ran through the door before they could stop me.

I ran down the block and around the corner toward Tarren's house, looking back over my shoulder the whole time in case they unleashed a fury of wraiths to come after me. Which meant I didn't see where I was going and I ran smack into someone in the middle of the sidewalk. I stumbled to the side, caught a glimpse of the army jacket, and fell over into the grass.

"Hey," I said, pointing up from my awkward spot on the ground. "You're Graham Goren."

Goren smiled, a little too self-satisfied. Then he offered me his hand. "That's me."

He pulled me up and I dusted off my butt. "I'm Josie," I told him. When this didn't seem to register, I said with more emphasis, "Josie Griffin!"

"Ahhh," he said. "So you're Josie Griffin—my tipster. Now this makes more sense." He held out his hand again, this time to shake mine. "Nice to meet you in person, Josie."

"Oh wow," I said like a starstruck fool. "I'm really excited to meet you." Then I looked over my shoulder again and I grabbed his elbow. "But I have to get out of here!" I looked around and spotted Gladys where I'd parked her earlier that day. "Come on. My car is right here."

chapter 17

get in," I told Goren when we got to Gladys. I shut and locked the doors, looking all around to make sure I wasn't being followed.

"Um," Goren said. "Mind if I roll down a window? It's a bit warm."

"But someone might hear us," I said. A bead of sweat rolled down the side of my face because it was about ten thousand degrees in the car.

He laughed a little. "I think we're safe."

"Suit yourself," I said and started cranking. "So much for having a discreet meeting inside a parked car."

"Were you just in Helping American Girls?" he asked.

"Yes and I heard your whole conversation. You're good."

He cocked his head to the side as if he was a little confused. "Thanks, I guess."

"I want to be a journalist, too."

"Ah." He pulled out his notepad. "So you know the first rule of being a good reporter."

"Don't bury the lede?"

"Nope. First, get all your facts straight."

I nodded, probably too enthusiastically. "Okay, here's what I've figured out so far . . ." but I stopped because obviously I couldn't tell him everything I knew. I tried to stick to the human-world facts. "Those two were lying. Those girls aren't out on the streets. I know a guy whose uncle runs the hood and he said the missing girls haven't been around."

Goren jotted a note but he didn't look convinced. "That doesn't mean they're not in a different neighborhood."

I hadn't thought of that, but still. "Yeah, only I know those girls and they aren't the type."

"You know them?" he asked. "Personally?"

"Yes, we're online together."

He frowned. "People can be different online. Computers depersonalize things so people feel free to make stuff up." He looked at me with raised eyebrows.

"Not us. We talked about all kinds of personal stuff. And also each of the girls who left were getting their lives together. Jobs. GEDs. Stuff like that. They had no motivation to take off without telling anyone. Not even their friends? Come on! Girls aren't like that. They tell each other everything."

"Maybe," he said. "But a boyfriend could have

showed up unexpectedly. Or a family member tracked them down. Did you contact anyone from the girls' lives and ask if they'd gone home?"

I sat back and bit my lip. "Well, no," I said. "The girls were hiding. They didn't want anyone to know where they were. They were running from terrible situations."

"Exactly," he said with a shrug. "They're runaways, so maybe they just kept on running."

"Without their stuff? What teenage girl would leave her favorite shoes and her cell phone behind?" I touched my back pocket where Sadie's ID card was nestled against my phone.

"You've got a point." He adjusted his glasses and wrote more notes. "Still, doesn't mean they wouldn't change their minds about being in a shelter. Teens get pissed off; do rash things they might regret." He looked up at me. "You know something about that, don't you, Josie?"

I shrugged, not sure what he was getting at.

"Tell me about anger management," he said.

My mouth dropped open. How did he know that? He saved me the trouble of asking. "Your trial was public record, you know."

"Oh," I squeaked. "That."

"Tell me about your blog."

"It's just something I do," I said, feeling cagey now. "Why? Have you seen it? Were you researching me?"

He raised one eyebrow. "Rule number two, Josie: Check out your sources."

"My blog is just a way to blow off steam." Despite the open windows, my palms began to sweat. "There's nothing wrong with that."

"I didn't say there was." He scratched the side of his head and thought for a moment. Then he said, "Tell me about your friends."

"The girls from the shelter, you mean?"

He shook his head. "The other ones."

"The cheerleaders?" I asked.

He shook his head again. "No, the other *other* ones."

My heart pounded in my chest and my underarms prickled in the heat as I realized that I had never gotten around to taking down my post about the paras. "Look," I said, trying to laugh it off. "If you're talking about my blog post from a few weeks ago, that was just silly. I was playing around. I mean, how many times can you post about a bad break up before it's just boring, boring, boring? I was trying to liven things up. It was stupid. Like you said, one of those rash things teens do online and regret . . ."

Goren looked at me now and I squirmed. "Josie," he asked, "are you a vampire?"

"A vampire?" I held out my hands. Made my eyes wide and innocent. "Don't be ridiculous. There's no such thing. I made all of that stuff up. You know how we teens love our paranormal stuff. You should just ignore that part."

"Right. What else should I ignore?" he asked. "The story about the missing girls?"

I turned quickly in my seat to face him. "No! That's true. For real. I'm serious. Those girls need help. Something weird is going on in that place. Ms. Babineaux and Maron are . . ." I stopped and chose my words carefully. "Up to something."

"Are they vampires?" he asked. I thought I heard amusement in his voice.

"No," I said and rubbed my temples. What was I going to do, claim there were soul suckers in that place after I'd denied everything else?

Goren closed his notebook. "Look, Josie, you seem like a nice kid who got a little mixed-up. Believe me, I had my share of mishaps when I was in high school. But being a journalist means you have to take the truth seriously. You can't make stuff up." He reached for the door handle and started to climb out of my car, but he turned back to me and said, "Unless you work for Fox News, then you can say whatever you want." He laughed at his own joke and closed the door behind him.

"Wait!" I yelled through the open window. "Are you going to write about the missing girls?"

"Nothing much to write," he said.

"I have a better source for you."

He bent down. "Who?"

"One of the girls," I told him. "She left and I know where she is. She knew everybody who disappeared. Personally."

He reached in his pocket and pulled out a card. "Give her this and tell her to contact me." He looked at me for a moment then he added, "And those other kids. The ones who think they're vampires and werewolves. Tell them to give me a call, too. I'd love to do a story on that!"

"But that's not even true!" I lied.

He snorted. "I'll tell you the real rule number one of journalism: Sell papers. And who wouldn't want to read about paranormal teens in an anger management group?" He laughed then walked off down the middle of the deserted street.

I slumped forward and groaned. I knew who wouldn't want to read about it. The Council, that was who. I banged my head against the steering wheel. So far that day, I'd forgotten to take down the post about the paras, falsely accused someone of pulling a knife, botched a reconnaissance mission to help my friend, and alienated the reporter who should be helping me. What else could go wrong? As I was banging away trying to figure out why I was such a screwup, my phone rang. Of course, I was hoping it would be Helios, the one thing that would make that crappy afternoon a little better. But it wasn't. It was my mom and she was pissed.

"Josephine," she said in that tone which immediately revealed I was in deep doo-doo. "I just got a call from your social worker."

I gasped. "Ms. Babineaux called you!"

"She said that you walked out of your shift today without finishing your work. Is that true?"

"No! I mean, I did walk out but it wasn't . . ."

"Josephine!" Mom snapped. "If getting arrested and going to court isn't enough to set you on the right path . . ."

"Mom, wait. You don't get it."

"Oh, I get it all right, Josie. Ms. Babineaux is threatening to send you to juvenile detention!"

"What?" I yelled. "That's not fair!"

"You better get yourself home right this instant. And you are not to leave again until we've worked this out and your father and I are satisfied that you will clean up your act. Not taking your community service seriously is serious business, young lady. I am seriously upset with you."

I refrained from saying, *Seriously?* "But, it wasn't even *really* my shift and . . ."

"I don't want to hear it," she said. "You are to come home right now."

"Okay, but first I have to . . ."

"Oh no. If you're not home in fifteen minutes, you will lose your car keys and your phone for a month. Are we clear?"

I knew when I was up against a wall and I definitely didn't want to be phoneless bus bait. "Fine," I mumbled. "I'm on my way." I hit the end button extra hard and threw my phone against the opposite door out of frustration. It ricocheted under the seat and immediately started ringing again. "Crap!" I slouched over and groped for it, among god-knows-what lurking on my car floor. By the time I got my fingers on it, I'd missed the call. "For crap's sake. What else could go wrong?" I muttered as I sat up and scrolled through my recent calls. But I was distracted by the tickle of a warm breeze on my neck. The hairs on my arms prickled and goose flesh flashed across my skin. I turned slowly, already wincing. I felt eyes on me. And hot sour breath. I turned to see a haunted face staring at me through the open driver's side window and I screamed.

chapter 18

damn these roll-up windows!" I yelled as I cranked and cranked and cranked the window up, but the pale, boney fingers gripped the top of the glass and I knew I'd never get the window closed. "Get away from me!" I screamed. I drew back my arm and balled my hand into a fist. "I'll punch you in the face!" I yelled, but I stopped after I got a good look at my attacker. I dropped my arm. "Eleanor?"

She stared at me, hollow-eyed and haunted, like a dog that's been abused, but she didn't say anything.

"What do you want?" My heart still raced. Maron could have sent this *chica* after me, but I was pretty sure I could take her. Unless of course she'd been imbued with superhuman strength and was going to reach in and squash my head like a ripe berry.

"I'm Ellie?" she said slowly.

"And I'm Josie. Are we really doing introductions

now?" Then I realized she was asking me a question and I softened. "Yes, you are Ellie, aren't you? Short for Eleanor?" I ask. "Who ran away from Elkhart? Jeez, sounds like a bad children's book."

Her eyes danced left and right as if she were scanning her memory. I tried to recall something else I'd read about her on the Missing and Exploited Children website.

"Your last name is Dellway, I think. You have a butterfly tattoo on your wrist."

She nodded, urging me to continue.

"You might have been a cheerleader," I said.

She blinked and opened her mouth, drew in a deep breath. "Help me," she pleaded quietly.

I looked at my clock. I had exactly thirteen minutes to get home. "I can't!" I said and started my car. But I felt kind of bad. I didn't have enough time to dump her off at Tarren's but if I left her on the street, Drey or someone worse would descend on her like flies on a dead raccoon. My phone buzzed from a new text. I reached for it, but Ellie reached in and gripped my shoulder. "Make it stop," she pleaded.

"Make what stop?"

Tears gathered on her lashes then rolled down her gaunt cheeks. "The evil one," she said.

I sighed. "Did it come to you in your dreams, sit on your chest, and drain your life force by any chance?" I asked.

She sucked in air and then wailed. I reached over and opened the passenger side door. "Get in," I said.

. . .

I pushed Gladys's pedal to the metal. Fat lot of good that did. Plumes of gray smoke farted from the tailpipe as we puttered through the city streets. Clearly the mechanic was no miracle worker. My phone was beeping and buzzing like crazy, probably my mom wanting to know why I wasn't home yet so I didn't answer. I banged my hands against the steering wheel and cursed every red light, slow driver, and pedestrian that got in my way.

At first, I tried to get some info out of Ellie. "How did you end up at HAG?" I asked. She stared at me in a stupid silence. "Do you live there?" She blinked. "Did you know Rhonda and Sadie? How about Kayla?" It was like someone pushed her mute button. "Aw, forget it," I said as we hit the outskirts of Broad Ripple.

When I turned onto my street, I inhaled deeply. I had no idea how I was going to explain this one to my parents. I started a runaway collection? I was only friends with freaks now? I guess that was what happened when you quit cheerleading and possibly uncovered a nefarious paranormal plot in your hometown. I killed the engine and turned to Ellie. "What am I going to do with you?" I looked all around our yard, then I saw my old playhouse. "Come on," I said. "You'll have to hide for a while."

Once I stuffed Ellie in the playhouse, I went inside. My parents descended the minute the front door closed. "What in god's name is wrong with you!" my father yelled. Once again I'd managed to make his forehead vein pulse.

My phone rang. I held up a finger and pulled my cell out of my pocket, but my mom swooped down like a red-tailed hawk on a limping vole. She grabbed it from me. "No!" she snapped. "Don't even think about it." She hit the OFF button and slammed it down on the credenza by the door.

"But I didn't do anything wrong!" I screamed at them.

"Have you lost all sense of reality?" my dad asked, and even though it was a rhetorical question, it was a good one because the boundaries of reality had slipped for me. The world had opened up and it was a darker place than it used to be. Old Josie had no idea what evil lurked in the world. I thought people were basically good and on my side. But the line between good and evil had become fuzzy.

"Look," I said, trying to stay calm and use some of the techniques Charles suggested. "I wasn't even scheduled to do a shift today. I went in on my own to help out. How can you not complete a shift you weren't scheduled to do? It makes no sense."

Mom put her hands on her hips. "Josie, do you understand that Ms. Babineaux has a lot of power over what happens to you?"

I snorted and muttered, "That's an understatement." Oops, guess I forgot the refrain from sarcasm rule.

"You might think this a big joke, but if you don't

follow through with your community service work at Helping American Girls, she could send you to juvenile detention," my father said.

And if did follow through, I thought to myself, I could end up with my brain sucked out. "I know I've disappointed you a lot lately, but . . ."

"That's not what this is about, Josie," Mom said. "We want to help you get back on the right track. We know you're a good kid . . ."

"I *am* a good kid!" I told them. "And you have to trust me a little. I'm trying to help some of the new friends I've made."

Mom and Dad exchanged a worried glance. "Listen, honey," Mom said in her all-too-understanding-mom voice. "At first your father and I were happy that you'd found some new kids to hang out with, but now we aren't so sure they're the kinds of kids you should be spending time with."

Dad leveled his gaze at me. "Maybe it's time to consider patching up your old friendships. School is starting soon and you don't want to be a loner . . ."

"Oh my god!" I said. "Are you actually suggesting that I should forgive Madison and Chloe? That I should be all buddy-buddy with Kevin? After what they did to me?"

"No, no," Mom said, her hands waving like surrender flags. "That's not at all what we're saying. But you've discounted lots of people. The other cheerleaders, perhaps."

"They all knew what was going on with Kevin and no one, not a single person, had the decency to tell me." I felt tears coming on, which pissed me off. I pushed them down. "My new friends might have lots of problems, but at least they've got my back."

Mom and Dad looked at each other then Mom said, "You've been acting differently lately. Not like the Josie we've always known. You're erratic and volatile. You've gotten in trouble with the law. It just makes us wonder . . . I mean, as your parents we can't help but worry that . . ."

"Josie," Dad said and cleared his throat. "Are you doing drugs with your new friends?"

This made me laugh. I was sure they'd been Googling "how to tell if your kid is doing drugs." As if that should be their biggest worry. "No," I said. "I don't do drugs. I never have and my new friends are *definitely* not druggies." And just then, as if the universe was on a mission to undermine me, the front door creaked open. Ellie stood on the threshold with leaves in her hair and grass stains on her knees, looking as strung out as a meth addict. Mom and Dad looked from her to me and shook their heads.

My parents and I gathered around the computer. Ellie sat across the table from us, staring down at her hands. I showed them her picture on the Center for Missing and Exploited Children website.

"You sure that's her?" Mom asked, looking from

the happy full-faced person on screen to the gaunt girl across from us.

"I think it is. Look at the tattoo," I told her.

Mom dabbed at her moist eyes with a tissue. "Ellie, honey," she said. "We really should call your parents and let them know that you're okay."

Ellie looked up with one of her signature blank stares.

"Can you tell us your phone number?" Dad asked.

She shook her head slowly.

"I'm sure they're worried sick," Mom said. "Her poor mother." Mom wrapped her arms around me and hugged me tight.

I figured that was about as good as it was going to get with my parents tonight. I hugged my mom back then I patted my dad on the shoulder. "Thank you so much for helping her. It's been a crazy day. I know I should have come to you first, but I didn't think you would understand. I was wrong. You guys are the best." See, Charles? I can suck up when I need to. Mom and Dad both smiled at me. "Do you mind if I take a shower while you track down her family?"

"Sure, honey," Mom said, blowing her nose. "Then we'll all have a nice dinner together."

"Sounds great," I said. "Mommy, do you think I could have my phone back?"

Without looking at me, Mom said, "Don't push it, Josephine."

"Okay," I said sweetly. "Never mind." And I shuffled

backward out of the room. In the doorway, I surveyed the scene. I felt kind of bad dumping Ellie on my parents, but then again, I didn't think she was dangerous. Plus it would be a great distraction for them to try to track down her family. I'd have a good twenty minutes before they missed me. I left the dining room and walked loudly up the stairs. I turned on the shower, then I tiptoed back down to the entryway, grabbed my keys and my phone from the credenza, and slipped out the front door.

Luckily when Kevin and I were together, I'd had plenty of practice rolling Gladys out of the driveway then jump-starting her half a block away. Once I got her going, I headed downtown. I had to find Kayla and the others and warn them that Ms. Babineaux and Maron were on to me.

chapter 19

Since Tarren's front porch was empty, I went straight to Buffy's. I'd never been there at night and the place was packed wall-to-wall with paras. I pushed my way through the crowd, looking for familiar faces, but the music was pumping and the lights were low so it was hard to find anyone. I did a double take when I saw a couple kids from my high school, someone I knew from summer camp, and a cheerleader from North Central. They each looked as surprised to see me. We exchanged slight nods like sealing a pact that we'd never divulge our dual lives outside the confines of this space. I wondered what they were—shape-shifters, vampires, elves, ogres, some other faerie tale creature I didn't know existed until a couple of weeks ago?

The first time I was in here, I thought it was all a joke, then I was scared, but this time I felt like I belonged. Toward the back of the room, I saw a knot of the love zombies all decked out in their skank robes. The more I studied them, the more I wondered whether they were trying to look just like the billboards for Zombie Apparel like my former friends or if they were the actual models in those ads.

Someone grabbed my shoulder. "Josie!" I jumped at first then relaxed when I saw that it was Avis. He pulled me through the crowd. "We've been freaking out!"

He dragged me to the table where Tarren, Johann, and Helios huddled over balled-up napkins and half-empty baskets of deep-fried everything. I was so relieved to see them that I ran and threw my arms around their shoulders. "Oh my god, you guys! It's been such a crazy day."

Tarren pushed me away. "Where in the name of Aine of Knockaine have you been?"

I stepped back, blinking in disbelief. "I . . . I . . . I . . ."

"You better tell me that Maron had you locked in a damn basement and you escaped," she said.

"No!" I put my hands on my hips. "But thanks for your concern."

"We called and texted a million times!" she yelled.

"Oh crap." I fumbled in my pocket and pushed the ON button on my phone. "My parents confiscated my phone, and I forgot that my mom turned it off." It buzzed and beeped and bonked at me with all the messages. "But why am I the only one getting yelled at?" I looked at Helios. "Where have you been?"

He sighed. "A minotaur ate my sister."

I blinked at him, trying to process that image. "Wait, what's a minotaur?" I asked, and dropped down in the chair beside Helios.

He looked exhausted. "You know, half man, half bull. Escaped from the labyrinth and went on a rampage, blah-di-blah-blah."

I put my hand on his thigh. "Is she . . . ?" I stopped, not sure what happens to one who's been eaten by a minotaur.

"Yeah, yeah, she's fine." He smiled weakly. "We got her back. No biggie."

"Jeez Louise!" I plucked a French fry from the basket and slouched back. "And I thought my day had been crazy." I looked around at everyone. They did not appear happy. "Hey," I asked. "Where's Kayla?"

Johann whimpered.

Tarren rolled her eyes but handed him a tissue and slung her arm around his slumping shoulders. "We were hoping she was with you."

"I haven't seen her since she swept Johann off his feet this morning," I said. "What happened after that?"

"We shared a delightful afternoon together," Johann said, dabbing at his eyes. "Paddleboating on the White River. A walk along the Monon Trail. Ice cream at BRICS in Broad Ripple. She loves the Yellow Cake Batter flavor. I was going to take her to a ballroom dancing class at Arthur Murray, but then . . ."

"You told us if we didn't hear from you two hours after you went into HAG that we should get worried,"

Avis said. "You never called or answered your phone."

"I'm so sorry. I couldn't! I feel terrible! This reporter showed up and Maron got suspicious and I had to ditch. Then Ms. Babineaux called my parents and threatened to throw me into juvie and I got in all kinds of trouble. One of the HAG clients followed me and I had to hide her and my parents think I'm on drugs and . . ."

"When we heard that you hadn't returned to Tarren's, Kayla vanished," Johann said.

"We think she went to HAG to look for you," Tarren said.

"Oh crap." I tossed aside the fries and held my head. "That's not good."

Johann slammed his hand on the table. "I shall avenge her!"

"Somebody's going to have to do something," I said. "Ms. Babineaux and Maron know we're on to them."

"Well," Tarren said all snippy, "while you were AWOL, that's what we've been discussing."

"Then what's the plan?" I sniped back.

"You two are as bad as Aphrodite and Athena with all the yap-yap-yapping back and forth," Helios said. "Man, I have had enough of women and their catfights."

"Look," said Avis, always the calm one. "We think Tarren should go to HAG and pose as a runaway to get in and find Kayla. The rest of us will surround the place and be waiting in case she needs help. It'll be easier now that we know Josie is safe."

"Thanks, Avis," I said. "I'm sorry you guys were

so worried about me. I almost feel like crying because you've been so nice to me. I almost forgot what it was like to have good friends." I took a deep breath so I wouldn't get all stupid-weepy, but for real, I was touched. "And of course, I'll do anything you need."

"I just wish we had more help," Avis muttered.

An idea came to me. I looked over my shoulder. "Them." I pointed to the love zombies. "They'll help us."

Just as we were getting ready to recruit the Johann fan club, the music faded and an unsettling murmur went through the room. Groups of people crowded around smartphones and laptops, pointing and arguing.

"What's going on?" Tarren asked.

"I'll find out," Avis said. He jumped up and perched on top of a table to get a better view of a group huddled near us while we tried to listen in on the conversations around us. I caught the words *demon hunters* and *the Council* and *extradition*.

"Somebody's in trouble," Helios said.

Avis came back to our group, nervously jutting his head forward and running his fingers through his red dreads that were nearly standing on end. "Looks like some demon hunter site figured out that Buffy's exists."

"There goes the only decent place to hang out," Tarren said.

Helios whipped out his smartphone. "I'm sure it's nothing." He pulled up the demon hunter site that Kevin was into, and we followed a thread from a bunch of semi-literate a-holes who barely knew how to spell.

**SHADOWSEER: This is the REAL DEAL! Demons
are amung us and they must be stopped b4 they
take over the world. Its dangerus work and this is
not a game. If u r a REAL demon hunter join us bc
we know were they r hidding.**
**FORENSICO: Ive been doing this work for long
time (10 yrs). I am not a wuss. Tell me where they
are and I will be there.**
B-AFRAID: I found this link. Its fer real.

"You guys aren't taking this seriously, are you?" I
asked. "I mean, even if some meathead dudes show up
here, what's the big deal?"

"Those kinds of idiots can be mean," Tarren said.

"Yeah, but you guys can just zap them, can't you?"
I said.

"A lot of people here are on probation," Avis explained as he paced around. "If we started zapping
these guys and word got out and the Council found out,
then all hell could break loose."

Helios clicked the link B-AFRAID mentioned and
Graham Goren's blog from the *Nuevo Ind*y website
came on the screen. My stomach dropped as my friends
huddled around to read the headline "Josie Griffin Is
Not a Vampire."

"Who the hell is Josie Griffin?" someone in the
crowd yelled.

I looked from face to face as my friends read the post. Panic filled my body. I started talking fast. "I never said I was a vampire."

Tarren was the first to look up. She was almost calm. "Did you rat us out?"

"No, no! I would never do that. This is just crazy. Graham Goren is supposed to be helping us—helping the girls."

As I tried to explain, the room grew more chaotic. The lights came up and people began pushing and shoving toward the door. "The humans are on to us!" someone yelled. "We've got to get out of here," someone else shouted.

"Come on, you guys," I pleaded. "You said yourself that nothing on the Internet about paras is real so why take this seriously?"

Johann stared at me, his eyes as black as the pit in my gut. "What exactly are you?"

"I'm your friend!" I said, fighting back tears because I knew what it felt like to be betrayed. Only this time my friends thought I was the betrayer and that horrified me. "I would never jeopardize you!"

"Are you a para at all? Are your parents?" Avis asked as he rocked back and forth, scratching at the floor with one foot and then another like a rooster getting ready to attack.

"There's a link to her blog," Helios told them. He held out his phone and I saw that Graham Goren, my hero, had linked to my blog. Helios clicked it and up popped my para post, the one I never got around to deleting.

"Look, you guys," I reached out, beseeching. I had to make them understand that it was all a mistake. "That was when I barely knew you. I never said who you were. And I was going to take it down. Besides, when I wrote it, we weren't even friends yet!"

Helios stood up. The bright light illuminated him from behind. He glowed, beautiful in his anger. Tarren, Avis, and Johann rose up beside him. They all looked down at me, cowering in my seat. "No," he said with an eerie calm. "We were never friends."

I covered my head with my arms, expecting a hex, a curse, sharp teeth, some kind of superhuman butt kicking to commence. But something far worse happened. My friends all turned away.

Helios led them forward into the crush of people heading for the doors. "We need to go. She talked about Buffy's in her post. Practically gave them a map of how to get here. It's only a matter of time before the DH find us and then the Council will not be far behind."

I tried to follow, begging my friends to forgive me, but I was pushed back by desperate arms and legs looking for a way out. The cheerleader from North Central caught my eye. She bared sharp fangs and howled at me, but a guy who was morphing from a preppy football player to a hairy beast yanked her through the throng with him. The crush in the stairwell was suffocating, but when I finally reached the open level of the parking garage, what I saw was as beautiful as it was heartbreaking and terrifying.

All around me, the flood of people shifted, their true natures drawn out in crisis. Some lifted off, black angels against pale yellow clouds. Others scurried, disappearing into the shadows of the night. Small clusters joined hands and ran, pulling each other one way or the other, fear flashing in their eyes. Most piled into cars and took off before the doors were even closed. A few simply faded away, their edges blurring into the gray air until they were gone. I stood in the center of the chaos, a wicked wind whipping through my hair. "I'm sorry!" I yelled at the top of voice. But no one paid attention.

As the garage cleared out, I heard tires screech, an engine gunning up the ramp. Headlights swept across the love zombies who wandered aimlessly among the pillars. An old black Chevy, the grill shining like shark's teeth, led a brigade of cars. The car skidded in a half circle and stopped in front of me. I saw the word *Impala* glitter under the weak fluorescent bulbs overhead. Two guys jumped out in the shadows then more people followed out of the other cars. "Where are they?" someone yelled at me.

I wrapped my arms around my body but I stood tall. "Who?"

"The demons! The freaks! The vampires and werewolves!" they screamed at me and advanced slowly into the light. "Are you one of them?"

I knew that voice. My jaw dropped and I put my

hands on my hips. "Kevin?" I said, totally annoyed. "What do you think you're doing?"

He stepped into the light. A brand spanking new black leather jacket creaked as he shielded his eyes against the light overhead and blinked at me. "Josie?"

"So it is you. I should have known," I said. I looked at the other guy. "Byron?" Kevin's best friend stepped into the circle of light.

"Oh hey, Josie. How's it going?" He shoved his hands into his pockets. "Haven't seen you around in a while."

"Oh really?" I said. "Wonder why."

The others murmured behind us. Kevin held up his hand. "It's okay," he yelled. "I know her." Then he looked at me. "You shouldn't be here."

"I can be wherever I want to be, jerkwad." I walked around him and peered into the car. "Who else is with you?"

Kevin hung his head. "Aw, come on, Josie. Don't."

I turned and glared at him. "Scared I might hurt your pretty new car?" I ran my finger along the shiny black paint.

"Hardly," he said, but the quiver in his voice and the fear in his eyes gave him away.

"You should be," I told him.

"She's not even here and you should leave," he said. "This place isn't safe."

"Says who?" I asked.

"I have my sources."

"Your sources are full of crap," I told him.

"How would you know?" he asked then he paused. "Unless . . ."

"Unless what?"

"You're one of them."

I shook my head. "Don't you read the news?" I asked. "I'm not a vampire."

Byron grabbed Kevin by the arm. "Come on, man. Every time we follow a lead from that demon hunter list-serv it turns out to be bogus. Let's go to Steak 'n Shake already."

Kevin stared hard at me for a moment. He lifted his arm and pointed at me. "Behold the wretch—the miserable monster I created!"

I rolled my eyes. "Save it for English lit, idiot. This has nothing to do with you."

Byron grabbed Kevin's arm and pulled him toward the car. "False alarm!" Kevin yelled to the crowd. The others got back into their cars and revved their engines. I stood my ground as they backed out. Their headlights swept across the love zombies who'd now formed a loose huddle off to the side. Kayla.

I knew I had to get to HAG before it was too late. I ran for my car but the love zombies stood in front of it. "Oh for god's sake, get out of the way!" I yelled at them but they didn't move. I yanked open all the doors. "Then get in you useless zombies!" I growled at them. "Get in before I kick your butts!"

As Gladys squealed out of the parking garage, we passed a long line of white, unmarked vans with tinted windows driving in a slow procession down Jefferson Street. I watched them in my rearview mirror as they turned into the parking garage. "The Council?" I asked the six girls piled in my car. They all looked at me blankly, of course. "Isn't there anything you guys know or can do to help me?" I yelled out of frustration but I got nothing in return. "Fine," I muttered. "I guess I'll still have to do this all myself."

I parked in the alley behind HAG. "Does this place look familiar to any of you?" I asked, but the love zombies didn't move, didn't talk; they just sat there staring straight ahead. I had no idea what to do and no one to help me. For the second time in my life I felt completely and utterly abandoned. Only this time, I deserved it. I laid my head against my steering wheel and fought back tears that threatened to explode from my eyes like a stupid geyser, but then I heard a familiar loud squeak. I squinted out the window and saw the lid to the Dumpster in the HAG parking lot sticking up. A shadow tossed a bundle into the Dumpster then the lid dropped with a loud *thunk*. I watched the shadow go back inside HAG. Once I heard the door close, I got out of the car and ran, half crouched, across the parking lot, stopping once behind a smoky gray Prius for a moment.

Fearing that Maron or Ms. Babineaux would pop out of the back door and grab me any minute, I sprinted to the Dumpster and threw open the lid. Peering down, there was just enough light for me to see a pair of green and blue Pumas, a duffel bag, and a tattered copy of *Pride and Prejudice and Zombies.* "No," I said aloud. "No, no, no." I fumbled for my phone and punched in Kayla's number. I heard the ring, muffled in the layers of trash. "No!" I shouted. "Oh, Kayla! No!" I heard someone wailing, the saddest cry of desperation I'd ever heard and then I realized that was me, crumpled on the cement with my head against the greasy side of the Dumpster.

I knew I had to shut up. I knew I had to leave, but I couldn't. I cried for my friend. For how I had let her down. For all the problems I had caused to the few people who'd been decent to me lately. I cried loud and stupid, like a blubbering idiot, until I felt the cold grip of bony fingers on my shoulder and I froze.

chapter 20

get off me!" I yelled and thrashed, throwing wild punches into the air, but not connecting with anything.

"Mmmh," the girl said. She tugged at me with the strength of a hummingbird trying to lift a dead horse. "Mmmh," she said again.

I scrambled to my feet and looked into the face of Bethany, the love zombie Kayla had freaked out over. She put her bony hand around my wrist and led me to the alley where the other zombie girls waited in a huddle. They seemed agitated, shifting from foot to foot, and making little moaning noises until Bethany and I joined them. They surrounded me then all at once they started to walk, heading north.

"But Gladys," I said, spinning around, trying to work my way against the tide of bodies. "We could just drive, you know!" They ignored me and continued walking, pushing me forward with their determined momentum.

We walked through alleyways and backyards, across railroad tracks, and under overpasses filled with trash. I had no idea where they were leading me and I didn't really care because at that moment, they were literally the only friends I had in the world. Zombies. *Nice*, I thought, *real nice. One more rung down the social ladder for me.*

After twenty minutes, I knew exactly where we were. The neat little houses and trim gardens filled with azaleas gave Lockerby away. "Oh no!" I said. "Are you taking me to Johann?" I tried to push my way out of the group, but they surrounded me again like we were a school of fish. Maybe Johann had been lying all along and they were his minions. "Are you doing his bidding?" I shouted, but of course, no one answered. They walked on, jostling to keep me in the center. "I won't go," I yelled at them. "You can't make me." I pushed hard against the girls until I broke their ranks and I slipped into the street. They stopped, cocked their heads to the side, and blinked at me with those horrible hollow eyes. I backed away, panicked, and scrambled into the shadow of a burnt-out streetlight then ducked behind a tall hedge in someone's yard.

Once I was out of sight, the girls turned away as if I had never been with them and continued their slow silent march down the street. I watched from a distance as they turned a corner then I decided that I should follow them.

I kept ten feet behind, lurking along the edge of the

sidewalk, ready to run away at any moment, but they ignored me. We turned another corner onto a street lined with big, old Victorian houses, only half of which had been fixed up. They trudged forward to the most run down of the houses. A single bulb burned weakly on the dilapidated porch and half the windows were boarded over. They marched up the steps single-file and vanished inside. I stood in the weedy front yard for a few minutes then I circled the house to get a lay of the land.

Behind the house, I saw the gray Prius from HAG. "Aha," I said, quietly confirming my suspicion that HAG and the love zombies were connected. But I still had no idea how. I thought of Kayla and Ellie and the girls. . . . Now I was too curious to let fear take over. I crept through the backyard, stepping over thorny bushes and patches of gravel to the back porch. The steps creaked under my weight, but I went slowly, sticking close to the rail that was protected by the shadow of a loose gutter hanging overhead. The porch ran the length of the back of the house and wrapped around the left side. I dropped to my knees and scurried up against the wall where I slunk from window to window, peering in each dark portal. The interior appeared to be black and empty until I got to the side of the house where a lamp burned in one of the rooms. I wrapped my fingers around the crumbling wood of the windowsill and very slowly inched up until I had a clear view of a large open space inside.

Love zombies filled the room. Some sat on ratty couches and ancient overstuffed armchairs. Others leaned up against the peeling wallpaper. A few lay on threadbare Oriental rugs in front of an empty ornate fireplace. I squinted, trying to find Bethany and the others who had led me away from HAG. I scanned each vacant face then I landed on a girl with thick blonde hair half-covering her features, but the butterfly shirt and short shorts gave her away. I stood up and slammed my hand against the pane. "Kayla!" I called. I grappled with the bottom of the sash and lifted. The window flew open. "Kayla!"

Movement in the corner of the room sent me ducking down out of sight. It was stupid of me to shout out—I had to keep control. When I peered into the open window again, I saw Atonia Babineaux weaving through the bodies. She trailed her fingers through their hair and along their arms as she slithered across the room. She looked like a snake taking its pick of drugged up rats in a science lab.

"Who will it be tonight?" she asked in a singsong voice. She stopped in front of a dark-skinned bag of bones slouched against the mantel. "You?" she asked and reached out to lift the girl's chin. Her cheekbones were as sharp as shale beneath a mass of unruly curls. She turned the girl's face left and right then moved on. "Or you?" She knelt in front of a girl with dyed blue hair who slouched, knock-kneed in a chair. Atonia spun around and crawled cat like across the floor, picking her way over arms and legs akimbo. "Perhaps someone new?" She stopped at Kayla and brushed the hair away from her face, which had been drained of all its vitality. Her blue eyes loomed large in dark sockets and her mouth looked like a gash across a stone. I didn't know what Atonia had done to my friend, but I knew I could take that skinny freak out if it meant saving Kayla. Except for one thing. Maron.

Maron marched into the room, barking, "It's all set!" She glanced toward the windows.

I jumped off the porch and sprinted across the yard. I had no idea if Maron had seen me half in and half out of the window or not, but I wasn't going to stick around and find out. I tore through the yards of Lockerby, hurdling flower beds and avoiding snarling dogs for three blocks until I tripped over a sprinkler and fell to my knees, gasping for air.

I had nowhere to go. No one to help me. The paras didn't trust me anymore. Neither did my parents for that matter. How long had it been since I snuck out? I was in way over my head. "What am I going to do?" I wailed up at the night sky, searching for some kind of answer but all I saw were the brightest stars glowing faintly through the haze of city lights. The Big Dipper, Orion's belt, Betelgeuse. The vastness of the universe weighed down on me and I whimpered.

I was the tiniest speck. Alone on the Earth on a late summer night. As insignificant as any bug. I lay back in the grass. There were no lights on in the house. No one to see me or ask what I was doing on their front yard. I realized at that moment, I could either freak out and lose my mind, or give up and crawl home to my parents who would surely be seething because by now they would have found the empty running shower and would be certain I was out trying to score some drugs for the half-zombie girl I dumped on them. Or I could I breathe like Charles had taught us in anger management.

After a few minutes, my heart had slowed and I could think again. Charles always said to break a problem down then deal with it step-by-step instead of rushing headfirst into more trouble. So. First step, I got up off the ground and brushed the grass off my knees and butt. Second step, I thought through all the people I could go to for help. Most of them I had to cross off. Tarren—she'd kill me. Helios—he would never have anything to do with me again. Avis—no matter how nice and chill he was, he would be loyal to Tarren and Helios. The Council—I had no idea who they were. My parents—they would never believe me, especially after I ditched tonight. Which left only one person who just might care enough to overlook what a jerk I'd been.

I got my bearings and headed for Johann's house.

I might have been stupid enough to ask a vampire for help, but I wasn't stupid enough to knock on his door and risk his mom taking a bite out of me. Instead I crept around the house, looking for a way to get his attention without disturbing his parents. I'd had plenty of practice sneaking around when Kevin and I first started dating, so I figured it shouldn't be too hard. I found a tree at the side of the house with some low branches. I picked up a handful of pebbles from the side yard and stuck them in my pocket.

"Jeez," I muttered as I hung by one knee from the lowest branch and tried to swing myself up. "My butt is getting too big for this." After about fifty tries I got on top of the branch. Then tree climbing came back to me like I was ten years old again. I worked my way from branch to branch until I was eye level with a lighted window. I straddled the branch and scooted forward so I could peer inside.

I don't know what I was expecting—a sarcophagus and blood-red velvet drapes? But Johann's room looked like every other guy's room I'd ever seen. A mess of clothes, posters of 80s bands, a desk with a computer, shelves of books shoved in at awkward angles. Apparently thirty years of being eighteen hadn't improved the slob factor much. I scanned the room for signs of life, or unlife I guess, and had almost given up when I realized that he was there, on the bed, lying so still that I had mistaken him for a mound of laundry. I took a pebble from my pocket and tossed it at the window. Nothing. I did it again. "Johann," I whispered harshly and threw more rocks. "Hey, Johann!"

He opened his eyes and rose from the bed like Bela Lugosi out of a coffin. "Johann! Come to your window."

Johann blinked a few times like he thought he'd

been dreaming, so I threw the rest of my pebbles, which startled him. He hopped up from the bed and thrust open the window. "Who's there?"

"It's Josie."

He found me among the leaves and glared. "*Gott im Himmel,* Yosie! What are you doing?" He frowned, "In a tree? At night. There could be bats out there," he said and squirmed.

"Please, Johann!" I pleaded as I realized what an idiotic idea climbing up there had been. He was a vampire. He could probably fly. But then again, he seemed to be afraid of bats. "Look, I know I messed up big time and you guys probably all hate me and rightfully so . . ."

"I'll never understand how humans can think we are the monsters," he said.

"You're right," I told him. "We're so much worse. But you have to believe me when I say, I never meant to hurt you guys or put you in any danger. I didn't know what I was doing. And I'm sorry."

He looked away. "Why are you here?"

"For Kayla," I pleaded. "I found her and . . ." Before I could get any more out, he slammed the window and dashed out of his room. "What the . . . ?" I wriggled across the branch to get a better look in the house, but then I heard the front door burst open and he was on the ground beneath me.

"Get down!" he commanded. "You will take me to her."

"Wow," I said, picking my way down through the branches. "I had a big speech ready with all the reasons you should help me . . ." I dropped down to the grass beside him and fell on my butt. "But that was easy."

He reached down, grabbed the back of my shirt, and lifted me to my feet as if I were a marionette. Then he pulled me close to his face. His black eyes glinted in the moonlight. I shuddered, fearing this would be my last breath before he drained me of my blood. "Shut it, Yosie," he growled.

"Okay," I squeaked. He dropped me like a cat that was tired of a dead mouse. I slumped to the ground then picked myself up. "Follow me."

We jogged three blocks to the big house and stood in the front yard. "She's in there," I said, pointing.

He put his hands on his hips and shook his head. "This is where the love zombies live."

"I know. It's like freakin' *America's Next Top Zombie* in there," I told him. "Plus that . . . thing that runs HAG and my crazy social worker are inside, too, but . . ." Before I could finish yammering, he was striding up the front porch steps to the door with superhuman confidence.

"Maybe we should think of a plan first!" I said, scurrying along behind him, but nothing was going to stop him. "Johann!" I whisper-yelled as I stepped into the eerie hall. "Johann, where'd you go?" I made my way toward the back of the house, past closed doors and a dark stairway. "We should really stick together, you know." I saw a light shining out from a half-open door. I took a deep breath and pushed it open.

Johann stood in the center of the room, half undressed and surrounded by desperate love zombies who clung to him, tearing his clothes from his limbs.

"Jeez, Johann," I said, stamping my foot. "Is this really the time to be getting it on with these zombie girls?"

"Yosie!" He reached for me like a man being pulled under water by piranhas. "Make them stop."

"Take me. End this. Free me," they moaned and pawed at him.

I stomped up and grabbed them by their skinny arms, tugging them away from him. "Okay, enough. Let go." But each time I got one off of him another would worm in between us and cling to him. "What do they want?" I asked, still yanking girls away.

"I don't know!" he cried.

"Bite me," one of them wailed. "Bite me!"

"You bite me!" I said and shoved her to the side. She fell like a crumpled sock then picked herself up and came at him again. "Can't you do something?" I asked Johann.

"Like what?" he said.

"I don't know. What would the Lost Boys do? Use your superhuman strength or turn into a bat or something!"

For a half second, he looked bewildered.

"I'll see why they're freaking out," someone called from the hallway. I knew that voice too well.

"It's Maron!" I whisper-screamed and ran to hide behind the door.

Johann closed his eyes, bowed his head, wrapped his arms around himself, and exploded. "Aaaargh!" he yelled and shook like a dog that just came out of a pond. Girls flew off his arms and legs and landed heaped in a perfect circle around his feet.

Maron stormed into the room, took one look at the strange guy and stopped. "What the . . . ?" she said, but Johann didn't waste any time. He turned and flew through the open window into the darkness of the night.

Great, I thought. *There goes the wimpiest vampire in the world.*

chapter 21

While Maron screamed at the lovesick zombies dragging themselves across the floor moaning for Johann, I slipped into the hallway. All I had to do was find Kayla and get us both out. That was it. Everybody else could fend for themselves. I had my own problems to deal with now. Namely Maron, who was still yelling at the zombies. At least she wasn't after me. Yet.

In the kitchen, I found a staircase leading to the basement. A light shone up the steps and I heard voices. Of course, I thought. Where else would the scariest people in the world be? Could they be in the dining room? No. Perhaps on the back deck having a nice cookout? No way. The only possibility was down the cellar stairs. If I were watching myself in a horror movie, I would call me an idiot and tell me to get out now. But I couldn't do that, because my friend was down there and she needed my help.

I searched around the kitchen for a butcher knife or a heavy candelabra to clobber someone with, but other than a wobbly table and a few broken chairs, the room was bare. Apparently love zombies didn't throw dinner parties. So, without a weapon or a plan, I did the only thing possible (besides peeing in my pants)—I went down the stairs.

"Turn her a little to the left," a man said, then a flash went off. "A little more." Another flash. "Push her head to the right." More flashes. "Yeah, like that. That's right. Work it, baby. Work it, girl."

I pressed my body against the dank cement wall and slowly crept forward. Between me and the voice were racks and racks of clothes. Mesh hoodies. Tiny tube tops. Plunging V-necks. Itty bitty micro-miniskirts and ripped-up fishnet hose. I scurried behind one of the racks and peered out through the hangers.

Huge lights illuminated a plain gray backdrop. A lanky guy with a frizzy comb-over and handlebar mustache clutched a camera. "Put some more girls in there," he said. "Like they're at a naughty slumber party." He leered and laughed.

Atonia moved bodies in front of the backdrop. She pushed and pulled them, turning legs out, setting one girl's hand on her protruding hip bone. She pushed another girl's forehead back until her chin tilted up and her mouth hung open as if she were in pain.

"Yeah, yeah," the guy said. "Just like that." Atonia got out of the way and he started snapping pictures again.

Kayla stood in the center. They'd charcoaled her eyes, teased her hair like she was going to the prom in 1982, and smeared blood-red lipstick across her mouth. She leaned to the left, her arms heavy at her sides, her head dangling and her mouth half open. The other girls slumped over her like rag dolls trying to hug. They were all eyes, hair, pouting mouths, elbows, knees, and hip bones in the same hideous purple dress with black slash marks across the belly that Madison had worn to my trial. I silently gasped and pressed my hand against my mouth. It worse than I imagined. They were being forced to model Zombie Apparel!

"Some guy got in the house!" Maron shouted, as she clomped down the stairs behind me. "He had them all in a frenzy."

Atonia and the photographer stopped the shoot and turned around. I was trapped and there was no place for me to go but inside the clothing racks, like a little kid hiding in a department store. I ducked and tried to climb inside the racks, but my foot got caught and I fell. Hangers clattered, fabric ripped, I sprawled face-first into the center of the floor, covered in trashy dresses. Nobody moved. Everybody just stared at me. So I stood up and tossed aside the clothes clinging to me. "Hey, Ms. Babineaux!" I said. "What a coincidence."

Atonia blinked, trying to make sense of everything. "Did you . . . ?" She looked at Maron but pointed at me. "Is she . . . ?"

"I don't know what she's doing here," Maron said.

"Just thought I'd help out!" I said and started cramming skirts and shirts back onto the rack.

Maron glared and came at me like a bull. I faked left then ran right and grabbed a rack of clothes. I spun it around and pushed as hard as I could toward Maron. It caught her in the boob and she stumbled off balance. As she careened sideways, clutching her right breast, I knocked over three more racks of clothes. "Run, Kayla! Run!" I screamed and dashed up the stairs. I exploded out of the stairwell into the kitchen and lurched around the corner where I hit a wall of girls. They packed the hall, moaning and shuffling.

"Move! Move! Get out of the way!" I yelled as I tried to push through them, but they were stacked three wide and five deep and drawn forward by some invisible force. I turned and ran the other way, into the kitchen again, still screaming for Kayla to get a move on. I barreled across the room toward the murky moonlight of the back porch. I reached for the door. I fumbled for the lock. I yanked and clawed at the metal, but something held me back. Hands around my waist dragged me down and pulled me to the floor. My knees crashed against old linoleum. I grappled for a corner of a cabinet, but something jerked me backward. I was flat on my belly being hauled against my will with my fingernails scraping across the floor. "No! No! No!" I screamed. "Help me! Somebody help me!"

Maron rolled me over on my back in the center of the kitchen. She huffed and snorted above me, her red hair shooting from her head like flames as she pinned my arms to my side. "Get off me, you fat cow!" I yelled as I thrashed and bucked. My knee connected with her kidney and she howled. I did it again and again until she let go of me and rolled off, writhing in pain. I struggled to my feet and came face-to-face with Atonia.

"You get away from me," I warned. "I don't know what you are or what you're doing, but you're not going to get away with it!"

She didn't speak. She just kept coming, slowly, steadily, silently. The doorway to the hall was still choked with zombie girls. Now the stairwell was clogged with the photographer and the girls coming up from the photo shoot. And between me and the back door was Maron, who'd managed to get to her feet, although she was clutching her side and breathing hard.

As Atonia got closer to me, I took a swing at her, but she was quick. She ducked and I missed. I ran in a circle and swung at her again but, like a cobra, she moved the top half of her body out of my reach then righted herself and kept advancing. I'd never been in a fight. Never taken a martial arts class or self-defense. There was only one way I knew how to use my body.

I counted in my head, *Five, six, seven, eight.* I clasped my hands in front of my chest, then reached into a high V above my head, I bent my knees, swung my arms, and just as Atonia lunged for me, I sprang, kicking my right leg forward and my left leg back in a hurdler jump. My toe caught her in the center of the chest and knocked her back. She stumbled, stunned. Blinking at me.

When she got her balance, she gasped for air and said, "Was that a cheerleading jump?"

"Yeah!" I said, pumping my fist. "And there's more where that came from!"

Atonia stood up straight and shook her head slowly.

"You shouldn't have done that," Maron said then she laughed. "We hate cheerleaders."

"Join the club," I told them, readying myself to jump again.

In the fuzzy gray light I could see a change come over Atonia. She ducked her head against her chest, rounded her shoulders, and collapsed in on herself. Then the top of her scalp beneath the spiky black hair split open and peeled back. A shrunken, shriveled wretch writhed forward out of the shell of her body. Sparse tufts of gray hair stuck out from her bulbous skull. Her nose, a pointed beak, thrust forward sniffing at me. She opened her mouth, revealing rows of crooked, razor-sharp fangs.

"Holy crap!" I said, paralyzed with fear. "I didn't see that coming."

Neither did the photographer who gaped at the wretched creature and ran screaming for the door.

"Aw, you stupid ninny," Maron yelled. She swiped, trying to grab him, but he wriggled past her, out the door and she made no move to chase him.

I looked back at the miserable creature Atonia had become. Wings unfurled from her shoulder blades and she flew at me. I threw my arm in front of my face then hit the floor before I knew what happened. "Sleep," she rasped, reaching for me with bony claws. "Sleep." Her claws dug into my collarbone and my body grew heavy, as if I had been suspended in thick, liquid amber.

"No," I moaned. "No." I couldn't move beneath her enormous weight perched on top of my chest, but I could feel her draining something from me. Taking it for herself. My childhood slipped away. Mornings, snuggled in my parents' bed, my tiny feet finding a warm spot behind my mother's knee. The smell of peanut butter toast and hot chocolate with marshmallows melting, steam thawing my frozen nose after sledding. My grandmother showing me how to pluck ripe black raspberries from the vines behind her barn, the taste bursting in my mouth, and then a pie cooling on the wire rack while we squeezed fresh lemonade. Aunt JoJo running alongside me, cheering me to pedal faster and hold on tight as she let go and sent me coasting on two wheels.

My first kiss. Kyle McIlhaney, red hair and freckles, tasted like barbecue potato chips and I pushed him away. Holding hands with Jarrett Duran, the first time my heart truly fluttered and how much I sweat when we went into the closet for Seven Minutes in Heaven at Chloe's sixth-grade birthday party. A new girl in eighth grade. Geeky in her braids and retainer, slurring all her *S*s. Madison. I didn't laugh. Invited her to the pool. We played Sharks and Minnows and ate Laffy Taffy then pinky swore to be best friends forever because who else would love "Hollaback Girl" and the Chronicles of Narnia as much as we did?

Atonia was draining it all from me, feasting off my memories and taking my life force for her own, sucking me dry like she had all the other girls. She would leave me a zombie, stuck between life and death, begging Johann to end the agony by sinking his fangs into my flesh. But I didn't want to die. I had too much to do. Too many things left to accomplish. I fought to open my eyes and when I did, I saw a beautiful thing.

Johann, Helios, Avis, and Tarren burst through the back door.

Helios pointed to me. "Get off of her!" he yelled, and the electricity surged. Every bulb in the house snapped on and the ceiling fan began to spin.

Atonia screeched and retracted her claws from my body. I scrambled backward, gasping for breath as Tarren rushed in, waving her arms and yelling, "I'll whip your clings, you bugly itch!"

Atonia fluttered for a moment, as if trying to figure out what Tarren meant but Maron saw an opening and charged.

"Tarren, look out!" I tried to yell. It came out barely more than a croak, but it was enough for Tarren to spin around and see Maron rushing toward her.

Tarren pointed to one of the broken chairs across the room. She raised her arms and the chair levitated then she flung it toward Maron. The chair zipped through the air as Tarren yelled, "Blushing crow!" The chair transformed into a large black bird that looked strangely embarrassed to be in the room. "Crushing blow! Crushing blow!" Tarren yelled, but it was too late. The crow flapped away through the open door. Tarren held out her arms to block Maron and screamed, "Hop stag!" Maron jumped and in midair morphed into a deer with huge antlers. The stag cleared Tarren's head and landed in the center of the room, confused and angry.

Atonia screeched and rocketed forward. She sank her sharp talons into Tarren's shoulders, but Tarren refused to go down. "By the strength of ten thousand faeries!" Tarren yelled. "You'll never take me." The wraith flung Tarren across the room, but she didn't smack into the wall or fall to the ground because the strap of her tank top caught the edge of the spinning ceiling fan blade. She hung from the whirling fan like a faerie-shaped piñata, screaming obscenities and daring Atonia to come back for her. "Bring it, you hazy crying flag. I'm not done with you yet!" she yelled as she twirled.

"Baby, I'm coming!" Avis yelled. He ran forward, furiously high stepping into the center of the room, which startled the stag. It reared onto its back legs and ran for the door.

"Helios! Johann! Stop her!" I barked, but they both ducked out of the doorway as the stag charged. She hurtled into the dark night and we heard her hooves clattered against the pavement outside.

I looked back at Avis, whose head jutted and arms

flapped. I cringed and covered my eyes, half afraid to witness his transformation into a wolfman. Then I noticed that he'd sprouted what appeared to be black feathers over his body. His shoes and clothes peeled away as his arms became wings, his toes grew webs, and his face morphed into two beady eyes and a bright red beak under a flopping cockscomb on the top of his head.

"You're a were-chicken!" I croaked at the mad-flapping rooster on the loose.

The feathers around his neck splayed forward as he jumped and crowed around the room, chasing Atonia who flapped from wall to wall, dive-bombing our heads. The zombies ducked, I hit the ground, and Helios crouched with one arm up, but Johann lost his mind. He ran across the room, waving his arms, squealing like a little girl. "Shoo! Shoo! Get away! Get away from me!" he screamed. Atonia grazed his head, followed by a squawking, flapping Avis. "It's in my hair!" Johann screeched and frantically batted at his head as he ran into the zombie girls at the top of the steps. They enveloped him, moaning and begging, pulling him down the stairwell like an undertow. "Kayla!" he yelled. "Kayla, help me!"

"Johann!" came a muffled cry beneath the flailing arms and legs. Then zombie girls were flung from the doorway like useless rags. Kayla and Johann emerged, arm in arm, triumphant in their reunion. But Atonia plunged at them. Johann squealed and clung to Kayla. Together they thrust across the floor as if they were dancing the tango. Atonia swooped again and Johann threw his body over Kayla in an epic dip. They rolled across the floor and landed under the rickety table.

I pushed up to my hands and knees, trying to find the strength to fight for my friends but I was still woozy and weak. I looked to Helios. Our last remaining hope, but he hadn't moved from his crouch, one arm shielding his face as if he were paralyzed with fear.

Atonia flapped up to the ceiling and hovered over me, claws out, teeth bared. "Josie!" someone yelled. I turned to see Kayla standing tall. She looked different. Not exactly like herself, but no longer zoned out like the zombies. Her eyes shone and her skin glittered. She grabbed the table and snapped one of the legs off like it was a toothpick then she threw it to me. I snagged it midair.

I felt the weight of the wooden leg in my hands and I planted my feet. "Come on!" I screamed, my voice now strong. "Bring it, you evil hag!" Atonia plunged at me claws first. I pulled back on the chair leg and swung as hard as I could. *Thwap!* The wood caught her squarely in the jaw and sent her tumbling backward across the floor. I tightened my grip and ran for her. Atonia looked up at me and bared her fangs. She hissed and spread her wings, but before she could lift off the ground I swung again and landed a blow on her sternum.

Pffff! Her body exploded like a vacuum cleaner bag full of dirt. A million tiny particles drifted in the air and covered all of us with a fine, powdery dust. We coughed and sputtered, manically trying to brush the dust off of us, but it absorbed into our skin. I tingled, from the inside out as the memories of my childhood rushed into my body again. One by one each of the zombie girls shuddered, shook, and reanimated, inflating like balloons on a helium tank.

"What happened??" "Where am I?" "What's going on?" they asked as they came to.

"Kayla!" I called. I searched for her in the bedlam and found her standing beside Johann, an eerie glow to her skin and eyes. "Kayla," I reached out to her. "Are you okay?"

Johann covered his face and wailed, "I was weak!"

My hand flew to my mouth. "You didn't."

Slowly, sadly, he nodded. But Kayla smiled, her incisors gleaming. "He set me free," she said. "Just as I asked him to."

"Oh hells no," Tarren said as she spun. "This is a truttload of bubbles."

As soon as the words left her mouth, tiny floating spheres filled the room. Raining down softly from the ceiling, our hair and clothes and the floor were quickly covered with thousands of sudsy bubbles.

"What in the name of Zeus!"

We all turned around. There in the doorway stood the most gorgeous woman I had ever seen. Her black hair, shining like polished onyx, tumbled over her shoulders and down her back.

"Mom!" Helios shouted, then the lights went out.

I was mesmerized by the woman illuminated in the moonlight. Rays of sun seemed to emanate from her hand as she searched the room. Then I realized, it wasn't sun rays at all. She was holding a flashlight. The bubbles created prisms in the light and made little rainbows dance over Avis, still in chicken form, scratching and pecking at the floor. Tarren spun slowly above our heads as the ceiling fan came to a stop. "Hi, Thea," she called down. The former zombie girls wandered around the room in their skanky clothes that were then four sizes too small. They laughed and joked as they poked the bubbles and wondered what kind of crazy party they'd all been at.

Helios's mom turned the flashlight onto him. He cowered in its glow. "Your text said people were in trouble here. I left my dinner party. I called the Council. But this . . ." She swept across the room with her light again. I dropped the chair leg. Johann quickly stepped away from Kayla. Avis's feathers had molted and he'd morphed back into human form. "Oh no, not again!" he said, covering himself with both hands.

"This looks like you're having a party!" Thea said.

"God, Mom," Helios said, stamping his foot. "You never believe me."

chapter 21

Once we had Tarren down from the fan and some clothes thrown together for Avis, we all gathered in the living room and tried to explain everything to Thea. It took a solid fifteen minutes to get the story out, but by the time the line of white Council vans started pulling up in the driveway, she seemed convinced that we'd done the right thing.

"Well," said Thea. "That's quite a story. However, I don't believe the Council needs to know all the details." She looked from Tarren to Avis, Johann to me, then to Helios. "What they don't know won't hurt them and I can make sure they know just enough to count you all as heroes."

We let go a collective sigh of relief.

"Except for you," she said, pointing to Johann. "You broke one of the most sacred laws. You changed a human."

Kayla stepped forward from the shadows and wrapped her arm around Johann's shoulder. "It was my choice."

Thea scoffed. "He took advantage. You were in an altered state."

"I knew exactly what I was doing," Kayla said. "I wanted this almost as soon as I met him."

Johann blinked at her. "You knew?"

Kayla nodded. "Yes, that first day, I knew what you were."

"But how?" he asked.

Kayla looked to me.

"My blog?" I cringed then buried my face in my hands. "It's all my fault," I moaned. "I'm so sorry." I looked up at Johann, expecting to be met with hate, but his eyes were kind.

He put his arm around Kayla's waist. "Without you, Yosie, I would have never met my destiny. How can I be angry?"

"Oh, Johann," I said sadly.

"I chose to be changed," Kayla said. She pushed up her sleeve and held out her inner arm. Two red puncture marks on the blue veins stared out like beady eyes. "After he ran for me in the kitchen, gallantly evading that horrible wraith, and we rolled across the floor in love's embrace. . . ."

"That's not the way I remember it," Tarren said half under her breath.

"I put my arm in his mouth and begged to be bitten," Kayla said.

"But he did the biting," said Thea. "The Council has very strict laws about that. I won't be able to intercede."

"What will happen to them?" I asked.

Thea looked grim. "I don't know. We haven't had a case like this in a very long time. But whatever it is, it won't be good."

"What if we leave?" Johann asked. "Right now. Take our chances in Saskatchewan as a young married couple?"

"Johann?" Kayla squealed. She threw her arms around his neck and jumped for joy. "Are you asking me to marry you?"

Johann stepped away. "What, huh, whoa . . ." he sputtered. Then he snorted. "I'm from a different era. 1980s East Berlin." He held her at arm's length. "If I'd met you then, we would have gone to the discotheque. Maybe had a picnic with our weekly ration of hard salami. Then later, after we applied for our one-room apartment, then perhaps . . ."

We heard doors slamming in the driveway.

"You have to go," I pleaded with them. "Before the other Council members get here."

"Mom?" Helios said.

Thea pressed her lips together. "If perhaps I were to walk out to the front porch to greet the Council and when we returned Johann and Kayla were no longer here, I would have forgotten them completely." She turned and strode slowly out of the room.

I was the first to throw my arms around Kayla and Johann and I begged them for forgiveness. "I'm so so so sorry. It's all my fault and I . . ."

"Yosie," Johann said, patting my back. "It's okay. Kayla and I are meant to be together."

Kayla snorted and stepped away from him. "Yeah, only you have no intention of marrying my butt."

"Ah, *liebchen*, you're only seventeen," said Johann.

"For the rest of my life," Kayla said.

He ran his finger down the side of her face. "We have eternity together," he told her.

She softened. "Where's Saskatchewan anyway? Down south?"

Johann pulled her to his side. "Don't worry," he assured her. "We'll get some very nice boots and warm coats. Maybe we can start a little business there, selling moose jerky."

"Here." Helios held out his keys to Johann. "Take my car. It's parked out back."

Johann looked stunned. "Are you sure?"

"It's just a car," Helios said with a shrug. "I can get another one."

"Can you get one for me?" Tarren asked.

Johann took the keys then hugged Helios. "You are my brother." They parted ways. He hugged Tarren then Avis. "I will miss you," he said.

"You sure?" Tarren asked.

"Eh," Johann said. "A bit anyway."

"You be safe now," Avis told him.

Then Kayla stepped forward. We all took turns hugging her, except for Tarren who stood back, thumped her hand against her heart and whispered, "Blood," as she tried not to cry.

Kayla grabbed her and pulled her against her chest like a little girl hugging her favorite doll. "You can come visit us anytime," she said.

We heard the front door open then heavy shoes against the creaking wooden floor.

"Go," we told them and pushed them through the open window. They flew across the backyard and left silently in Helios's chariot. When we turned around, Thea had come back. We could hear other voices in the hall.

"Where are all the girls?" she asked.

"I think they're all in the basement," I told her, "getting a new wardrobe and trying to figure what the heck they're doing here."

"Hmmm," she said, pondering. "How are we going to explain that one?"

"What will you do with them?" I asked her.

"Ah, leave that one to me," Thea said. "We will take excellent care of them. I have plenty of experience setting troubled girls on the right path."

Helios leaned over and whispered, "You've never met my crazy sisters. These girls are nothing compared to Selene and Eos."

. . .

Tarren, Avis, Helios, and I stood quietly on the front porch and watched as Thea ushered Bethany, Rhonda, Sadie, and the other girls into the waiting Council vans. After they pulled away, no one said anything. We stood in silence for several minutes, awkward together after everything had happened. Then the rev of a loud engine filled the street again.

"Who could that be?" asked Tarren.

"Oh crap," I said when I saw a black Impala speeding toward us. "You guys should get out of here."

"What is it?" Avis asked.

"My dip head, douche hat, dumb hick, demon hunter ex-boyfriend," I said.

Kevin drove up over the curb and into the yard, his fat tires digging ruts in the dirt. He jumped out and stood in the glare of his headlights. "Looks like your luck has run out, demons!"

"Oh for crap's sake, Kevin," I yelled at him. "Would you get a life already?"

He shielded his eyes and squinted. "Josie?" he said. "Is that you? Again? Jesus, I can't get away from you tonight."

"You're the one who's following me, you idiot," I said.

He put his hands on his hips. "Jeez, Josie. I know you lost your mind when I broke up with you, but this is just pathetic. How did you get mixed up with these freaks?"

I looked to my left at Tarren and Avis, and to Helios on my right. How did I get mixed up with them? Did

Atonia Babineaux mean to send me to that first anger management meeting, or did I just walk into the wrong place?

Tarren stepped forward. "First of all, jerkface," she yelled at Kevin, "you never broke up with Josie. She broke up with you when she bashed in your freakin' windshield."

Avis joined Tarren. "And watch who you're calling a freak!"

Kevin took a step forward and pointed. "These people are not what you think, Josie!"

I crossed my arms and stood tall. "Yes, they are," I told him. "They're my friends. Which is more than I could have ever said for you or any of the cheerleaders."

I felt an arm around my shoulder and looked up to see Helios standing beside me in a sudden surge of light. "I think it's best if you leave now," he told Kevin calmly. "You wouldn't want your new car to get damaged." He clenched his fist, set his jaw, and stared at Kevin's car. The engine revved, the lights blazed brighter, and smoke poured out of the tail pipe.

Kevin jumped. "What the . . . ?"

I laughed. "Don't you have some slut to go screw?"

"This isn't over," he yelled as he scrambled into the driver's side. "We're on to you." He peeled out, spitting dirt and weeds behind him as he fishtailed down the street and around the corner.

"That guy is seriously douchey," Tarren said.

"How could you ever have dated him?" Avis asked.

"Clearly her taste in men has improved considerably," Helios said.

I stared at all three of them. "Um, does this mean you guys aren't mad at me anymore?"

They looked at each other. Tarren spoke first. "I'm still pissed at you," she admitted. "I mean, you did totally out us on the Internet. That was a jerk move."

"Then why did you help me?" I asked.

"Johann came to get us," Avis said. "And like we told you when we first met, we have each other's backs."

"Even mine?" I asked, astonished.

"Well," said Helios. "It helped that we read your blog posts and realized that you actually said nice things about us and that you cared about what was happening at HAG. All that pep talk stuff you do is for real."

I blushed at the thought of Old Josie coming through so strong, but then I realized it wasn't such a bad thing to be enthusiastic and persuasive about the right cause.

"Plus whatever you wrote about us couldn't be that big of a deal," Avis said. He grabbed Tarren's hand and they started down the stairs. Helios and I followed. "I mean, only idiots like your ex-boyfriend take that stuff seriously. Everyone else thinks it's a joke."

"Humans!" Tarren said and laughed.

"But still, I lied to you guys. Doesn't that make you mad?" I said as we turned onto the sidewalk.

"Perhaps we're all learning to manage our anger better," Helios said.

"Charles would be so proud," Avis snorted.

"Yeah, right." Tarren cracked up. "We were the picture of control in there." She pointed back to the house—now just another rundown Victorian on a quiet Indianapolis street.

"Dude, you're a were-chicken!" I said to Avis.

He laughed. "Better than a werepire."

"Got me there," I said.

Tarren laid her head on his arm. "I thought you were awesome."

"I froze like a Popsicle," Helios said. "But Josie kicked some serious butt."

"Yeah, girl," said Avis. "You got a mad swing."

I laughed. "I think I might go out for softball."

"Thank god," said Tarren. "I don't think I could hang out with you anymore if you were a cheerleader."

A little thrill went through me at the thought of hanging out with the paras during my senior year. Then I remembered. My parents. I still had to face their wrath. But still, it couldn't be worse than what we'd just gone through. They'd understand, eventually. I hoped. "I'll probably be grounded for the rest of my life, so I might not see you for a while."

"That's okay, we'll come to your house since you managed to shut down Buffy's," Avis said.

"Oh no," I groaned. "I'm so sorry!"

"Don't worry about it," Helios said. "It's happened before. It'll relocate soon."

We turned a corner and walked side by side under the gently glowing streetlights of Lockerby while somewhere Johann and Kayla were cruising into a new life up north.

The next morning we would read about a kid who totaled his vintage Chevy Impala when he struck a deer that bounded into traffic on I-465. The kid would have a concussion, which would explain his ramblings about demons, but the deer would die. Those Zombie Apparel billboards would fade away by the time school started in two weeks, replaced by yet another ad campaign the mindless fashion drones would follow. And as for the rest of us, we had four more weeks of anger management to go.

Turn the page
to read the first chapter
of Heather Swain's

ME, MY ELF & I

chapter 1

"ARE YOU LOST?" The man is big. Bigger than any other man I've ever seen in my life and for a moment I can't say anything. My grandmother, back in Alverland, would call this man an ogre, even though he's the only person out of all the people rushing past me in this subway station nice enough to notice that I'm completely confused.

Everyone else just jostles on by, jabbing me with elbows and banging me with overstuffed shoulder bags. I feel as if I'm caught in the middle of a moose stampede during a forest fire. (Only instead of being surrounded by burning trees, I'm in a smelly underground passage with dirty walls covered by advertisement posters for a million things I've never heard of.) I hug my bag to my chest and nod without making a sound. The man leans down closer to me. It's not just that he's tall. I'm used to tall people. Everyone in my family is tall. He's also wide, soft, pillowy. I think of sinking into my grandparents' large goose-feather bed with my brothers and sisters and cousins surrounding me, anticipating my grandmother telling us a tale about giants and ogres.

The man's skin is dark, too, and I'm captivated. Everyone in Alverland is fair. Our hair is light and straight and our eyes are almost

1

always green. Drake, my father, who's been out of Alverland more than anyone else, told us that there are many kinds of erdlers (that's what we call people who aren't from Alverland) and you can judge them based only on their actions, not on how they look. So I know I shouldn't stare at this guy. Or any of the people rushing past me. Especially because I know how it feels to be different.

"Where are you trying to go?" he asks.

It's bad enough that I took the wrong subway three times. I mean, how was I supposed to know? I'd never even ridden a bus before today. But now that I'm finally at the right station, I can't find my way outside. I unclutch the piece of paper wadded in my fist and show it to him. I clear my throat and try out my voice. "The Brooklyn Academy of Performing Arts High School," I tell him, but the words come out tiny, as if I'm six years old. Great, my first time alone in Brooklyn and I can't even talk like a regular fifteen-year-old girl. How will I ever make it through a day of high school?

He takes the paper from me and studies it with a frown. "Never heard of it," he mumbles, and I think he'll walk away, leaving me stranded forever. I wonder if I give up now, could I find my way back to our house near the park? Tell my mom and dad that they were right. I'm not ready for a regular school. I should let them teach me at home like they wanted to in the first place.

Then the man looks up and nods. "But I do know this street, Fulton Avenue. Come on. I'm walking that way. I'll show you." He takes off and I hesitate. Everyone back in Alverland warned us not to talk to strangers, never to go with people we don't know, and to keep to ourselves. But this guy has my paper with the school's address on it. So I force my legs to move and I skitter after him, weaving through the rushing people in this dingy underground passage.

He leads me to a stairway and I can see sunlight again, although the air doesn't smell any cleaner up there than it does down here. I press my sleeve over my nose and mouth to keep from gagging on the car fumes. He takes the steps two at a time and I run to keep up with him. He glances over his shoulder and smiles kindly at me.

"New to the city?" he yells over the roaring traffic. I see him chuckle.

"Yeah," I yell back, defeated. "First day of high school."

"Sheez." He shakes his head. "Rough start. But it'll get better." He points to a street packed with cars, trucks, motorcycles, blue-and-white buses, and bicycles. A flood of people spill out of the underground stairways. Like ants on a mission, scurrying over rocks, past sticks, through gullies just to get their crumbs, the people keep moving along the crammed sidewalks, across the streets, and into the hulking buildings surrounding us. He and I join this throng and I realize that his size is a plus because at least I won't lose sight of him. On the opposite corner he stops and points. "This is Fulton Avenue. The address says four thirty-six, which has to be down this way on the left side. If you get lost, ask somebody. New Yorkers aren't rude. They're just in a hurry, but somebody'll always help you if you ask." He hands me my piece of paper and walks off into the crowd.

"Thank you!" I yell after him. "Thank you for helping me!" I wave my paper over my head as he disappears beneath the shadows of skyscrapers. Then I'm alone again in the middle of hundreds of people. For a moment I consider zapping everyone around me with a hex, maybe some kind of skin pox or limping disease of the knees so that they'll all fall down moaning and I can step over them, one by one, as if walking on rocks across a stream to find my way to school. But of course I don't. First of all, I'm not really old enough to hex an entire crowd of moving people, and secondly, my mother warned me, No magic in Brooklyn!

* * *

I finally find the school, but I'm late, of course, even though I left my house hours earlier. In Alverland, nothing is more than a ten-minute walk away, so spending this much time getting anyplace seems absurd. Standing in the middle of the empty hallway I wonder why I insisted, fought, begged, bartered, made promises, and endlessly cajoled my parents into letting me attend public high school in a new place. Am I out of my mind? Did somebody put the donkey hex of stupidity on me? I thought this was going to be easy. All I'd have to do is dress like an erdler and I'd fit right in. As if I could waltz into this school, playing my lute, and everything would be fine. Obviously I'm an idiot.

I'm about to turn around and head out the big green doors of the school. Back into the chaotic, smelly street, where I'll probably wander around lost for years before I find my way to the subway, let alone all the way home. I'm about to chuck it all, tell my parents they were right, and hole up for the rest of my existence in my new cramped bedroom at the top of the stairs in our house, when someone says, "Why are you out of class?"

I turn around to face a tiny, angry woman scowling at me. She has small sharp features like a mouse. Her hands are balled into fists, which she holds on her hips like weapons. Plus she's wearing all green. She looks just like the mean little pixies my grandmother used to tease us about. "I said, what are you doing out of class? Do you have a hall pass? What's your name?" the pixie lady demands.

That's when I lose it. Lose it like a snot-nosed, diaper-wearing, thumb-sucking, toothless, babbling baby. I drop my bag to the floor, let my knees go weak, slump over into a heap of quivering jelly, and cry miserably. The pixie lady stares me down while I wail. I swear she checks her watch and taps her foot impatiently until I pull it together enough to lift my head and squeak, "I don't know where to go."

She rolls her eyes. "Do you always get this worked up when you're lost?"

I suck back the snot streaming down my face, wipe my hands across my moist eyes, and say, "I've never been this lost before."

"For God's sake, girl," she hisses. "You're inside a school. How hard can it be?"

This only makes me cry harder, because I know she's right. "But I, but I, but, but . . ." I sputter. "First the trains . . . and I went the wrong way . . . was it the F or the A or the 2 or 3 . . . and who can figure out those maps with all the colors? Red! Blue! Orange! How was I supposed to know which platform, which staircase, which end of the train I'm supposed to get on? Not to mention the subway stations! There are rats down there. And it smells. Terrible. And all those people? Where are they all going? Where could so many people be going?" I come out of my rant clutching my hair and stamping my feet as if I'm having a temper tantrum, which, actually, I am.

The pixie grabs me by the upper arm and pulls. I scoop up my bag and go tripping behind her. "How many drama queens can one school hold?" she mutters to herself as she drags me down the empty hall.

We pass closed doors through which I hear teachers' voices over groups of kids laughing. I also hear music (drums, pianos, a trumpet from far away) and feet stomping in unison as if dancing. Posters cover the walls inviting me to "Join Student Government" or "Come to the First Chess Club Meeting Tonight" or "Help Plan the Halloween Dance!" I drag my feet to slow the pixie down so I can read every flyer on a large bulletin board. This weekend there's going to be a film festival and an "open mic night," whatever that is. And today after school I could go to a free talk about poverty in Africa or even learn how to crochet. I could never do those things in Alverland, but here, I can do anything, and that's why I came today.

The pixie stops and I bump into her, nearly sending her to the floor. "Good God!" she says to the ceiling. "Not even nine o'clock yet and this is my day already." She points to a half-open door and gives me a little shove. "In you go," she says. "Tell it all to the shrinky dink, drama queen."

I'm inside a bright, sunny office with a wilting jade plant in the window and sad yellow daisies in a vase. Without thinking I whisper one of the first incantations my grandmother taught us, "Flowers, flowers please don't die, lift your heads up to the sky!" Slowly the jade plant unfurls its drooping leaves and the daisies stand tall in the vase. Then I remember that I shouldn't be casting spells, no matter how harmless. What if someone saw me? How would I explain? I consider undoing the incantation, but that would be more magic. I have to be careful now. I must remember to act like an erdler.

I hear quick footsteps in the hallway. I peek out the door and see a couple hurrying by, holding hands. The girl's hair flies over her shoulder as she looks up at the guy. "We're so late," she says, and they both laugh, then they're gone around a corner.

I'm left with a tingly feeling in the pit of my stomach. Before my family left Alverland, my cousin Briar and I spent hours in the branches of a sycamore tree, talking about how erdlers fall in love, date, fight, and break up with broken hearts. Or so we've heard.

"Do you think you'll have a boyfriend there?" Briar had asked me a hundred times.

"That's not why I want to go," I told her as I picked layers of shaggy bark off the peeling tree trunk. "I just want the chance to see another part of the world, try new things, eat food I've only heard of." But secretly I wondered if I would find an erdler boy in Brooklyn. Then again, I can barely find my way to school, so how will I ever find a boyfriend? I need to focus on the real reason I'm here: music, art, experience! All of the things missing in Alverland.

I drop onto a little couch and try to regroup. I need to break the problem into manageable steps, as my mother likes to say. I take a deep breath and try to remember My Plan for Life in Brooklyn. First, make friends. (But how?) Second, get a boyfriend. (Yeah, right!) Third, and most important, find as many ways to perform as possible. I have one year here, and I'm not going to waste it.

I look around the office again. Beside me on a little table is a big black binder titled "Upcoming Auditions." It's filled with dozens of pages with information about trying out for plays, musicals, bands, ensembles, improv troupes, and commercials. I get prickly chills up and down my back. *This is it!* I think. The real reason I'm here. In Alverland we do the same pageants and plays every season—to welcome in the harvest, to give thanks for bountiful hunting, to celebrate the equinox. It's always the same songs, in the same order, on the same day. Nobody writes plays about a different topic or makes up new songs except my dad. It's not that I don't like singing in the sugar shack when we make syrup for the Festival of Maple Trees, but there's more to life than pancakes!

As I browse through the binder of possibilities, a door across the room opens and a woman walks in. She's too preoccupied with reading the paper in her hands to notice me, so I take a second to get a good look at her. She wears a full, rippling purple skirt with tiny bells sewn on the hem that jingle as she moves. On top she wears a long flowing white shirt, not unlike what we wear in Alverland. She has three necklaces of brightly colored beads, lots of bracelets on both wrists and even around one ankle above her soft leather sandals. She tucks a loose strand of her brown hair behind one ear and I see that she has silver rings on nearly every finger. I like her already.

"Are you the shrinky dink?" I ask.

"Yow!" she shrieks, and gives a little jump so that all her bracelets, necklaces, rings, and bells clink and clatter. "The shrinky dink?" she asks, as if she can't believe I said that.

"Sorry." I cringe. "That's what that woman told me." I point to the door where the lady in green left me, but of course she's long gone, vanished just like a mean little pixie would. "Am I in the wrong place?"

She narrows her eyes to study me. "Who are you?"

"My name is Zephyr," I tell her, then remember how the erdlers always use last names, too. "Zephyr Addler."

"Ah ha!" She grins. "So you are Zephyr. I've been looking forward to meeting you."

"You have?" I ask, and for the first time since I kissed my mom goodbye this morning, I smile.

She nods. "I'm Ms. Sanchez, your *guidance counselor*," she tells me carefully. I get the hint that "shrinky dink" is not what I should call her. I imagine how the pixie will look after I zing her with a nasty little hairloss spell for embarrassing me like this. Then I remember my no-magic promise to my mom.

"So you made it," Ms. Sanchez says as she perches on the edge of her desk.

"Barely," I admit.

Ms. Sanchez pulls a red file folder off her desk. I see my name printed on the tab. "So you've never been to a regular school?"

I shake my head, more embarrassed now. "I didn't realize everyone in the universe would know that about me."

Ms. Sanchez laughs. "Only your teachers and I know that about you. And you're not the only homeschooled student we've ever had. It's nothing to be ashamed of. Especially with test scores like yours."

"Thanks," I mumble. "But being smart hasn't stopped me from being an idiot today."

"Don't be so hard on yourself," she tells me. "It's tough coming to a new school as a sophomore, especially a week after everyone else started."

"Oh no," I groan and clutch my knapsack to my chest. She makes it sound so terrible!

"You're going to do just fine," she assures me as she flips the pages in the red folder. "Let's see where you're supposed be now and get you started."

Ms. Sanchez knocks on a classroom door and goes inside. I wait in the hallway but I hear people murmur, papers shuffle, and someone laughing inside the room. "Settle down," an adult says, then a girl comes out in the hall with Ms. Sanchez.

"What's up, Aunt Nina?" the girl asks. Ms. Sanchez frowns for a moment until the girl rolls her eyes and says, "Ms. Sanchez," in a silly voice that makes Ms. Sanchez snicker.

"Mercedes, this is Zephyr. Zephyr?" She turns to me. "This is my niece, Mercedes. She's also a sophomore here and she'll be your official tour guide today."

When Ms. Sanchez steps aside, Mercedes and I face each other as if we're looking in an opposites mirror. I am tall. She is short. I'm as pale as milk. Her skin is the rich, beautiful brown of acorns. My stick-straight, so-blond-it's-nearly-translucent hair hangs down below my shoulders. Her thick, dark ringlets are cropped just above her chin. I am all points and angles: cheekbones, collarbones, elbow, knees; she is soft curves from her round cheeks down to her feet.

And it's not just how we're built, it's how we're dressed. I've taken great care today not to look like some hippie wood sprite straight off the commune (which is what most erdlers think of us when we leave Alverland). I purposely left my soft deerskin boots and handwoven tunic dress at home. I didn't even wear my hat or the amulets my grandparents made for me. I gaze at Mercedes in her red-striped tank top over a white T-shirt and skinny jeans riding below her hips and pegged above her silver ballet flats. I realize I look nothing like a regular erdler kid. My navy blue pants are too fitted, too new, too stiff, too high up on my waist. I have on a bona fide blouse, aquamarine with pearly buttons all the way up to my chin. And I'm wearing white sneakers. I'm so embarrassed that I wish someone would turn me into a bird so I could fly away and never ever see these people again.

"My aunt told me about you," Mercedes says. "You're the girl from Michigan, right?"

"The U.P.," I say hopefully, but Ms. Sanchez and Mercedes look at me blankly. "See, Michigan has two parts." I hold up my right hand like a mitten with the thumb sticking out to the side. "This is the main part where Detroit and stuff like that is." I hold my left hand sideways over the top of my right fingertips. "And this is the Upper Peninsula, the U.P." They blink at me. "All this space between my hands is the Great Lakes. And up here?" I point to the pinky knuckle on my left hand. "That's where I grew up."

"Close to Canada then?" Mercedes asks.

"That's right!" I say, impressed with her grasp of geography. Most people in Michigan have no idea how close we are to Canada.

"Yeah," she says, smirking. "I can hear your accent. 'Out and about.'" She laughs because she pronounces it like "oot and aboot."

I press my lips together as my cheeks grow warm, embarrassed by how obviously weird I seem, even in this school where the brochure says diversity is a good thing.

"But that's okay, yo, because I'll have you talking Brooklyn in no time flat." Mercedes snaps her fingers in front of her face and grins at me, this time nicely.

Ms. Sanchez hands Mercedes a green slip. "Here's a hall pass. Show

Zephyr her locker, the cafeteria, her homeroom, then escort her to her classes for the rest of the day."

Ms. Sanchez turns to me. "You can stop by my office anytime if you have a question." She slips her arm around Mercedes's waist. "Mercy will be a great tour guide, won't you?"

Mercedes wiggles out of her aunt's embrace, but I see her smile. "Yeah, yeah, Aunt Nina."

"Ms. Sanchez," Ms. Sanchez says playfully over her shoulder as she walks away.

First I ask to stop in the bathroom so I can do something about how I look. I stand in front of the mirror and sigh. "I look like . . ." I say to Mercedes.

She sits on the countertop, kicking her feet into the big rubber trash can stuffed full of used paper towels. "A dork," she says. "Which is weird because, you're like, so freakin' gorgeous and everything. Does your mom make you dress like that so boys won't be looking at you?"

"No. I mean, I just didn't know what to wear." I untuck my shirt and undo the top button. I take off my belt and shove it in my bag. (A *belt*! She's right. I am a total dork.) I try to squiggle my pants down around my hips, but it's hopeless. "Is that better?"

Mercedes raises her eyebrows. "Yeah, better, but . . ." She hops down from the counter. "I don't know what kind of malls they have up there in the U.P., but girl, we're gonna have to take you shopping or something."

I follow her out of the bathroom. "Please," I beg. "I would really, really appreciate that."

Mercedes snorts a little laugh. "'I would really, really appreciate that!'" she mocks, and I have to give her credit, she truly does sound like me. "For real you talk like that?"

I stop and tower over her. "How am I supposed to talk?"

She shrugs. "I don't know. However you talk, you talk, I guess. It's sweet, kind of. Real nicey nicey. Polite sounding."

"Is that a bad thing?"

"Naw, just different," she assures me. "But maybe you want to tone it down a little bit with people you don't know. Otherwise, you know, they might get the wrong idea."

"That I'm nice?" I ask. "What's wrong with being nice?"

"Too nice. Like people can take advantage of you. Push you around. You know. Like that. You gotta be able to hold your own here."

"Right, hold my own." Then I realize that again I'm lost. "Hold my own what?"

This time Mercedes cracks up. She leans into me and shakes my arm as she laughs. "Girl, you crazy! 'Hold my own what?' " She imitates me perfectly again. "You really are from someplace else, aren't you?"

"You have no idea," I tell her. "No idea at all."